The " Teaching of English" Series

General Editor—Dr. Richard Wilson

FAMOUS FABLES

No. 193

FAMOUS FABLES

Collected and Retold by

F. B. KIRKMAN, B.A.

THOMAS NELSON & SONS, LTD.

LONDON AND EDINBURGH

ACKNOWLEDGMENTS

For testing both the fables and the questions in class, my thanks are due to Miss Newsham (Deptford Junior Girls' School); Miss Cora Robins; Mr. G. T. Brown and Mr. T. Fletcher (Lancaster Road Boys' School).

Acknowledgment is also due to John Murray for permission to include abridged versions of three of the stories from M. Frere's *Old Deccan Days*.

First published in this Series, September 1935.

CONTENTS

1. THE THIN CAT AND THE FAT CAT (*Indian*) .   7
2. THE LION AND THE OLD HARE (*Indian*) .   10
3. THE DEER, THE CROW, AND THE JACKAL (*Indian*) 13
4. THE MAN AND THE BEAR (*Indian*) . . . 17
5. THE CROCODILE AND THE MONKEY'S HEART (*Indian*) 22
6. THE LUCKY POTTER (*Indian*)* . . . 24
7. THE JACKAL AND THE ALLIGATOR (*Indian*)* . 29
8. THE TIGER AND THE PRIEST (*Indian*)* . . 34
9. STOP TO THINK (*Indian*) . . . 37
10. THE RATS AND THE BARS OF IRON (*Indian*) 39
11. THE MONKEYS WATER THE FLOWER-BEDS (*Indian*) 42
12. THE CRANE AND THE CRAB (*Indian*) . . 44
13. THE WEASEL, THE RABBIT, AND THE CAT (*Indian*) 47
14. ONCE A CAT, ALWAYS A CAT (*Indian*) . . 48
15. THE THREE ROGUES (*Indian*) . . . 50
16. THE SHEPHERD AND THE KING (*Indian*) . . 51
17. THE SQUIRREL, THE OWL, AND THE MOLE (*Burmese*) 54
18. THE TOWN MOUSE AND THE COUNTRY MOUSE (*Æsop*)† 56
19. THE HERON (*Æsop*) 59
20. THE FOX GIVES AND LEARNS A LESSON (*Æsop*) 60
21. THE FOX AND THE STORKS (*Æsop*) . . 64
22. THE HARE AND THE TORTOISE (*Æsop*) . . 67
23. COUNTING THE CHICKENS BEFORE THEY ARE HATCHED (*Æsop*) 69
24. THE WOLF AND THE DOG (*Æsop*) . . 71
25. THE GRASSHOPPER AND THE ANT (*Æsop*) . 72
26. THE GOLDEN AXE (*Æsop*) . . . 73
27. THE WOLF AND THE STORK (*Æsop*) . . 74
28. THE WOLF AND THE LAMB (*Æsop*) . . 75

* From M. Frere's *Old Deccan Days* (1868). † Greek.

29. THE LION AND THE MOUSE (*Æsop*) . . . 77
30. LOOK BEFORE YOU LEAP (*Æsop*) . . . 78
31. KING LOG AND KING STORK (*Æsop*) . . 80
32. THE SICK LION (*Æsop*) 81
33. SOUR GRAPES (*Æsop*) 82
34. THE FROGS AND THE OX (*Æsop*) . . . 84
35. THE EAGLE AND THE BEETLE (*Æsop*) . . 84
36. THE WISE LARK (*Æsop*) 86
37. THE CROW'S MISTAKE (*Æsop*) . . . 88
38. THE MONKEY AND THE DOLPHIN (*Æsop*) . 89
39. THE ASS IN THE LION'S SKIN (*Æsop*) . . 90
40. KILLING THE GOOSE WITH THE GOLDEN EGGS
    (*Æsop*) 90
41. THE BEAR GIVES A LESSON (*Æsop*) . . . 92
42. THE OAK AND THE REED (*Æsop*) . . . 94
43. PRIDE GOES BEFORE A FALL (*Æsop*) . . 95
44. THE MISERY OF MIDAS (*Greek*) . . . 95
45. THE MILLER GOES TO MARKET (*Latin*) . . 98
46. BELLING THE CAT (*Abstemius*) . . . 100
47. THE SAUSAGE (*English*) 102
48. CHANTICLEER AND THE FOX (*Chaucer*)* . 103
49. THE COLT'S LESSON (*Florian*)† . . . 105
50. THE SELFISH FRIEND (*Florian*) . . . 107
51. THE CORRIDOR OF TEMPTATION (*Voltaire*)† 108
52. THE WOLF WHO WAS AT OXFORD (*Renard the
    Fox*)† 110
53. THE WOLF HAS A LESSON IN FISHING (*Renard
    the Fox*) 111
54. THE LION, THE WOLF, AND THE FOX (*Renard
    the Fox*) 114
55. TOO CLEVER BY HALF (*Renard the Fox*) . 115
56. THE TORTOISE TRAVELS (*La Fontaine*)‡ . 116
57. THE HORSE-CLOTH (*French*) . . . 117
58. THE TWO FRIENDS (*Krylov*)§ . . . 119

QUESTIONS 121

    * Based on Æsop.   † French.
    ‡ From an Indian source.   § Russian.

FAMOUS FABLES

1. THE THIN CAT AND THE FAT CAT

A CAT lived with a poor woman in a hut. Like her mistress, she was half starved and very thin. She had long forgotten the taste of milk, and thought herself lucky if she was given a crust of bread. She seldom caught a mouse, for the few that came to the cottage left as soon as they found there was nothing to eat. She saw nothing of most of them but the print of their feet in the dust.

When the cat did catch a mouse, she would sit and look at it, touch it with her paw, and ask herself :

" Is this a real mouse, or am I dreaming ? "

She was never quite certain until she had eaten the mouse and felt less hungry.

" If I am less hungry," said she, " I must have eaten something, and so that mouse must have been a real mouse."

One day she was sitting on the doorstep. She was trying to think what it feels like to eat as much as one wants, when she saw a sight that filled her with wonder. There, along the top of the wall, walked a cat so fat that he seemed hardly able to lift one foot after the other. When the thin cat had got over her surprise she cried out :

" In the name of pity speak to me, O happiest of the cat kind ! Why, you look as if you fed every day from the table of a king ! "

" That is just where I do feed," said the fat cat, stopping. " I go every day to the king's table after he has dined ; I eat just what I like, and just as much as I like. When I leave, an army of mice come out from under the floor and eat what is left."

" Then, of course, you eat the mice," said the thin cat, smiling at the very thought of such feasting.

" Eat the mice ? " said the fat cat. " Why should I eat the mice ? Why on earth should I put myself to the trouble of eating the stringy flesh of mice ? Eat the mice ! Pah ! "

The fat cat gave a flick with one of his front paws as if tossing a mouse out of his sight.

For some moments the thin cat could say nothing ; she was so surprised that any cat could speak in that way of eating mice. Then she begged the fat cat to let her go with him to the king's house.

" Come along," said the fat cat. " You are as

thin as a rat's tail. Come along. We will soon change all that.''

Some minutes later they were on the king's table. They found on it what was left of a splendid feast.

The thin cat lost no time in beginning. She took several mouthfuls from the nearest dish, then ran to the next and took some from that, and then to a third, and so passed from dish to dish and from joy to joy.

All of a sudden a man with a stick bounded into the room. He shouted :

" Now I have you, you rascals ! "

The fat cat, being slow to move, got the first blow, and that was the end of him. The thin cat sprang out of the window on to the wall, but there another man struck her a blow that left her lying as if dead. The man, thinking he had killed her, went off.

He forgot that a cat has nine lives. His stick had knocked all the lives out of the thin cat except the ninth. The ninth was enough to go on with.

In time the cat came to her senses and crawled home. There she lay down, feeling very ill.

" Never again ! " she said. " Better a crust in a hut with safety than a feast in a palace with a stick round the corner ! "

2. THE LION AND THE OLD HARE

THERE was once a lion. He hunted and killed the other animals with such fury that they lived in terror day and night. At last they sent him a message. The crow was chosen to take the message because it was easy for him to keep out of reach of the lion's paw, if His Majesty lost his temper.

The crow found the lion at the mouth of his den. He said why he had come, and went on thus :

" The animals asked me to tell Your Majesty they are proud to have such a mighty lion as you for king, but they complain that you give them no peace."

" Well, I must eat," snarled the lion. " Do they expect me to live on air, or eat grass ? "

" No, Your Majesty," answered the crow. " They expect you to eat flesh. They are ready, indeed, to send you each day one animal to be eaten, if you agree to stop hunting them."

The lion agreed at once, for he saw that the plan would save him trouble.

" Mind," said he, " that my meals do not dawdle on the way."

From that time an animal went to the lion daily and was eaten.

One day it came to the turn of an old hare.

He did not at all like going to be eaten. The more he thought about it the less he liked it, and the more he wanted to go on thinking. He went on thinking, till there came to his ears a distant sound of angry roaring.

The hare rose and went towards the roaring. On the way he passed a cave in which there was a deep well. As his mouth felt very dry, he went in to drink. He got nothing, for the water was out of his reach, but he saw his own frightened face looking up from the well as from a glass. That put an idea into his head.

" It is not much of an idea," said he to himself ; " still, it may save my life."

He went towards the roaring, which grew louder and louder, and fiercer and fiercer.

When the lion saw the hare coming he stopped roaring, and snarled :

" What do you mean by keeping me waiting ? What excuse have you for not coming to be eaten at the proper time ? "

" He would not let me, Your Majesty."

" He ?   Who is ' he ' ? " asked the lion.

" That other lion," said the old hare.

" What other lion ? "

" The lion in that cave over there.   He called me and told me that from to-day the animals were to go to him to be eaten."

" Oh, did he ? " said the lion.   " Was that all ? "

" No.   He said also that I was to go to him
to be eaten after I had given you a message."

" Give it," growled the lion.

" I would rather not, Your Majesty."

" Give it at once ! " roared the lion.

" He said you were to get out of this country,
and be quick about it."

" What if I do not get out ? " asked the lion,
baring his teeth.

" He said, Your Majesty, he said . . . well, he
said that if you do not. . . . No, I would rather
not repeat what he said."

" Out with it ! " roared the lion.

" He said he would . . . drag you out . . . by
the tail."

At this the lion's mane stood all on end, so
great was his rage.   Springing up, he bade the
hare lead on, and, with long leaps, raced after
him to the cave.

On reaching it he rushed in, filling it with
roars, and the roars echoed back at him.

" That is he roaring," screamed the hare.

" Where is he ? " snarled the lion.

" Down that hole," screamed the hare.

The lion looked down the hole and there,
looking up at him, was another lion just as furious
and ugly as himself.   At once he sprang down ;
splash he fell into the water, and a few minutes
later he was drowned.

For the next quarter of an hour the old hare,

in his joy, danced all round the well, and rolled over and over on the grass outside ; then with great, springy leaps he went off and told the other animals the news. They were so glad, that they passed on the spot a law that any dog, wolf, fox, or other beast of prey that ever dared to hunt the old hare was at once to be driven into the cave and drowned in that same well.

3. THE DEER, THE CROW, AND THE JACKAL

A DEER and a crow were friends. In the daytime each went his own way to look for food, but in the evening they met and talked. When it was time to sleep, the deer lay down at the foot of a tree and the crow perched on a branch above him.

One day the deer met a jackal in the woods.

" Eh, what a fine deer ! " said the jackal to himself. " If only I could get him shot or trapped, what a meal he would make ! "

While these thoughts were passing through the jackal's head the deer stood still, looking at him, and wondering whether he was friend or foe.

" Good-day to you ! " said the jackal.

" Who *are* you ? " said the deer.

" I am Small-wit, the jackal, so called because I am said to have little sense. I live in the wood

here, alone, without a friend. In you I think I
see a friend. I feel as if I had known you all my
life. Let me be your friend."

" By all means," said the deer ; and both went
to the place where the deer was in the habit of
meeting the crow. When the crow saw them he
said :

" Who is this, friend deer ? "

" It is Small-wit, the jackal ! " said the deer.
" He wishes to be my friend."

" Is it wise to make friends so quickly ? " said
the crow. " You know nothing of Mr. Smallwit."

" Sir," said the jackal, " when you first made
friends with the deer what did he know of you ?
Yet are you not still his friend ? Let me be his
friend, and yours too."

" Yes," said the deer, " let us all three be
friends."

" Very good," said the crow, " as you will."
And so each evening there were three at the
meeting-place instead of two.

Some days later the jackal said to the deer :

" Deer, at one corner of this wood is a field of
fresh young corn. Come and let me show it to
you."

The deer found the corn very much to his
taste, and he went to the field morning after
morning. The farmer, seeing his corn eaten and
noting the prints of the deer's hoofs, set a net
trap. In this the deer was caught.

When the jackal saw that the deer was trapped, he was delighted.   He promised himself a splendid feast on all the scraps of deer's flesh that the farmer's wife would throw out.   The deer, for his part, on seeing the jackal, was just as delighted.

" Oh, how glad I am to see you, friend jackal ! " he cried.   " Come quick, and bite through this vile net and set me free."

The jackal went up to the net, looked at it closely to make sure it was strong and would hold.   Then he said :

" Dear friend, to-day is a fast day, and I have sworn not to touch anything with my teeth. To-morrow, if you still wish it, I shall be delighted to do what you ask."

Then off he ran.

That evening neither deer nor jackal came to the meeting-place.   The crow became alarmed, and, flying high into the air, circled over woods and fields.   Soon his sharp eyes noted where the deer lay.   Down he went like a black arrow.

" What means this ? " said he.

" It means," answered the deer, " that you were right, and that in my haste I made a false friend."

" Where is the rascal ? " asked the crow.

" You may be sure he is somewhere near, waiting for his share of my flesh," sighed the deer.

" Well, he is not going to get it," said the

crow; "but we will talk about that to-morrow morning."

The crow passed the night on a branch close to where the deer lay. He woke at sunrise, and the first thing he saw was the farmer, with a big club in his hand, coming over the field.

"Here comes the man," said he to the deer. "Pretend to be dead. Stretch out your legs straight and stiff. Do not move. I will perch on your head, and seem to be pecking at your eyes. When you hear me croak, leap up and run."

The man, thinking the deer was dead, drove away the crow, unfastened the net, and was folding it, when a sharp croak made him look up. There was the deer alive and bounding away. The man picked up his club and hurled it with all his might. The club missed the deer, but it struck—whom do you think? It struck Small-wit, the jackal. He was not seen in those parts again.

That evening, you may be sure, the crow and the deer had much to say. They talked till late into the night, and before they went to sleep the deer did what he had never done before, and never did again—he made up two lines of poetry. Here they are:

> "A friend in need
> Is a friend indeed."

4. THE MAN AND THE BEAR

I

A BEAR lived by himself in a big wood.   He lived alone because his wife was dead, and his children were grown up and had gone away into other woods.   He felt much more lonely than an ordinary bear would have felt : an ordinary bear cannot talk ; this bear could.   He would wander for hours among the trees seeking some one to whom he could say just a word.   He met very few, and these did not wait to hear more than the first words ; they could not talk themselves, and they thought there must be something wrong with an animal that could.

One day, as the bear was walking near the edge of the wood, he met a man.   Thinking he might be attacked, the man turned to run.

" Do not be frightened," said the bear ; " I am not an ordinary bear.   As you see, I can talk ; and I am very glad to have some one to talk to, for I live in this wood alone."

When the man had got over his surprise he said :

" Well, to tell you the truth, I also live alone, in that hut down there in the field.   I am very glad to have a neighbour to speak to.   Come along and have something to eat."

They went into the hut and had a good meal.

The man gave the bear what bears love—that is, honey. This he spread on thick slabs of bread; and the bear, when he had finished, took the honey-pot and licked it clean.

During the meal, and after the meal, they talked. They talked, and they talked, and they talked. They talked till they were quite tired, and then they went to sleep side by side in the garden.

The bear was the first to wake up. When he saw the man, the garden, and the hut, he thought at first that he was dreaming. Then he remembered what had happened. He looked at his friend again, and presently he noticed that he did not seem quite comfortable in his sleep: he was moving his head from side to side, and giving it little jerks.

On looking more closely, the bear saw that on the tip of his friend's nose there was a fly. As it walked about it tickled the nose with its feet, and it was that which made the man so uncomfortable. The bear drove the fly away several times, but each time it came back.

At last the bear grew angry, and said to himself: " If that fly comes again I will just catch it."

He held his great paw over the man's face and waited. In a second the fly was back. Down came the paw, but not quick enough. It just did not catch the fly. What it did was to flatten the man's nose, cut his lips and cheeks, and nearly break his front teeth.

Nobody could have been more astonished than the bear : he had been so eager to catch the fly that he quite forgot his heavy paw would hurt the man.   As for the man, he woke up with a cry of pain.

When he saw the bear leaning over him he thought, of course, that the animal had hit him on purpose, and felt very angry.   When the bear told him how it had happened, and how sorry he. was, he said :

" All right.   I see you really meant to do me a kindness ; I feel angry no longer."

They went into the hut.   The man bathed his face and went to bed.   As it hurt him to talk, the bear sat beside him and told him wonderful stories of the woods, till he fell asleep.

II

Next day the man was better, and after the midday meal the two friends again went to sleep in the garden.   When the bear woke up, the first thing he saw was the fly walking on the tip of the sleeping man's nose.   He drove it off several times, then said to himself :

" Now what *am* I to do ? "

After thinking the matter over, he went into the house to see if he could find anything to put over the man's face, but he found nothing.   He came out and went all round the garden, talking to himself as he went :

" What about leaves ? No, they are no use. What about earth ? No, it is no use. Pebbles ? No. Twigs ? No. Grass ? Why, the very thing ! "

So he pulled up some grass, went to the man, and arranged it round and over his nose. When the fly came back it found no nose to walk upon, but only what looked like a great green stack rising from the man's face.

The bear was just beginning to smile with pleasure when the tip of one of the blades of grass was drawn into the man's nose by his breath. The blade tickled the inside of the nose ; the man gave a tremendous sneeze, and away went the grass in all directions. The sneeze not only woke the man, it hurt his nose dreadfully. He looked angrily at the bear and said :

" What *have* you been doing now ? "

When the bear told him, he could not help laughing. " Well, it certainly was a splendid idea," he said, " and what happened only shows how hard it is to think of everything."

Next day they again went to sleep in the garden, but not till the man had said :

" Whatever happens, do not touch my face with anything."

When the bear woke up there was that fly

taking its usual walk on the man's nose. The bear looked at it crossly and said :

" Now what *am* I to do ? "

As he was thinking, he heard above his head a twitter. On looking up he saw a swallow, flying swiftly this way and that, catching flies.

" The very thing ! " he said, and then shouted " Hallo ! "

Now it happened that the swallow could talk. On hearing the bear's shout she flew down, hovered in the air in front of him, and said :

" Good-day, Mr. Bear. It is not the first time I have heard you speak. As you see, I can also speak. What can I do to serve you ? "

" Good-day to you, Mrs. Swallow," answered the bear. " It is very good of you to offer to do me a service, and I shall be glad to ask one. Look at my friend there. Do you think that, without touching his nose, you could pick off that . . ."

Before the bear could say " fly," the swallow had already swooped down to the nose. The fly saw her coming and took flight ; it had not flown an inch before it was snapped up. After that the swallow, whenever she passed, looked at the man's nose, and when she saw a fly there took it. Not one escaped.

The man was delighted when he heard what the bear had done, and was very grateful. The two went on living quite happily together.

5. THE CROCODILE AND THE MONKEY'S HEART

" I AM ill," said the crocodile's wife. " Only one thing will cure me. The doctor told me so. If you love me, you will get it."

" What is it, my dear ? " asked the crocodile. " If it can be got, you shall have it."

" A monkey's heart."

" A monkey's heart," cried the crocodile. " How on earth am I to get a monkey's heart ? "

" How should I know ? " said his wife. " What I do know is that if you don't get it, I shall die."

The crocodile went off to think. He lay like a log, and thought hard. It was easy enough to find a monkey. There were plenty in the trees by the river ; but between finding a monkey and getting his heart there was all the difference in the world. What was he to do ? He thought and thought till his head ached, for he was not used to thinking. At last he had an idea. He went to a fir tree by the river-side, in which there lived a monkey.

He greeted the monkey, and said :

" I wonder why it is you stay on this side of the river when there is far more to eat on the other side."

" Why wonder ? " said the monkey. " The

reason is clear enough. I cannot get across to the other side. If I could I would."

"Oh, is that all?" said the crocodile. "Well, I am going across to the other side now myself. If you hurry up and get on my back I will take you across."

The monkey said he would be only too glad. He thanked the crocodile, and jumped on his back. When they were half-way across, the monkey saw that the crocodile was sinking. It was not long before he was himself half under water.

"What are you doing?" he cried. "If you go on sinking like this I shall be drowned."

"Well, why not?" said the crocodile, with a long, toothy grin. "The doctor says my wife must have a monkey's heart to eat. She is going to have one. She is going to have your heart; and soon."

Just think what the monkey's feelings were on hearing that. Still, he kept his head.

"It is a good thing you told me," he said calmly. "Do you think I carry my heart about with me?"

"Of course," said the crocodile.

"Then you are mistaken," said the monkey. "If I went jumping about in the trees with it inside me, it would soon be broken. It is far too precious to break—as your wife knows."

"Well, where is your heart?" asked the crocodile.

" It is hanging in the tree where I was."

" I must have it," snapped the crocodile.

" By all means," said the monkey. " You can have it in return for taking me across the river."

" I must have it before I take you across."

" All right," said the monkey; " but only because Mrs. Crocodile is ill."

The crocodile returned with furious haste to the tree. The monkey leapt off his back and was up among the branches in a twinkling. Then he turned and said :

" You are not so clever as you think, you stupid crocodile. My heart is inside me. It always has been ; and it is going to stop there. You can tell your ugly old wretch of a wife that I am not going to lose my heart to her."

The crocodile's wife was so angry when she heard the monkey's message that she got well there and then, and raged and raged all round the pool, lashing the water with her tail.

6. THE LUCKY POTTER

I

IT was night ; the rain poured down in floods, the thunder rattled, the lightning flashed, the wind screamed. Through the jungle came a tiger ; it was trembling with fear, and looking for a place to hide. It saw a hut, and crouched down against the wall.

Inside the hut was an old woman. The tiger could hear her moving about and talking to herself :

" Oh dear ! Oh dear ! This dreadful drip, drip ! I shall be wet through if it goes on—drip, drip, drip ! I would as soon have a tiger in the hut."

The tiger asked itself what this dreadful drip, drip could be that was worse than a tiger. As it lay wondering, a potter came running and stumbling through the darkness. He was in a furious temper, for he had lost his donkey. A flash of lightning showed him what seemed to be the donkey crouching against the wall of the hut. He rushed up to it, shouting :

" What do you mean by leaving me, you wretch ? Get up, or I will break every bone in your body."

He began to kick and beat the tiger with all his might.

" This must be that dreadful drip, drip," thought the tiger. It got up at once, feeling it best to do what it was told.

The potter drove it before him with kicks and blows all the way to his house. Then he tied it to a post, and, with a parting kick, went indoors to bed.

Next morning the potter's wife woke him up ;

she was in a state of great excitement, and cried :

" Do you know what you brought here last night ? "

" My donkey, of course."

" Oh, did you ?   Just go and see."

On opening the door the potter saw a tiger fastened to the donkey post.

" Well, I never ! " he cried.   " How on earth did I manage to do that ? "

He could find no answer. It was not long before the news of his deed spread all over the country. Everybody believed that the potter had, with his own hands, caught and tied the beast up, for it could not, and would not, have tied itself up. As every one wanted to make his tale more exciting than any one else's, the fame of the potter grew and grew.

II

Not long afterwards the potter's king went to war with another king. After much fighting, the other king won a great victory. The potter's king did not know what to do. At last some one said to him :

" Why not make the brave potter general of your army ? A man who can catch a tiger with his hands can do anything."

The potter was then and there made general of the army, and the king sent him the finest war-horse in his stables.

When the potter saw the horse, he said to his wife :

" What am I to do ? I shall never be able to keep on its back."

" Leave it to me," she said. " We will get up early, before any one is about ; I will do the rest."

Next morning, while his wife fed the horse with lumps of sugar, the potter climbed on to its back from a chair. Then he sat and patted its neck, while she fastened him on with a strong rope. The horse soon had more rope than it cared for ; after kicking and plunging, it went off at full gallop, with the potter clinging to its neck.

The potter did not like being tossed about on the horse's back ; and he liked his ride still less when he saw that he was being taken straight to the enemy's camp.

" I must get off somehow," he thought.

As he could not untie the ropes while he was being tossed about, he saw that he had first of all to make the horse stop. He took hold of a young tree as he passed and kept hold ; but the tree came up by the roots, so he dragged it along, hoping to tire the horse out.

When the soldiers in the enemy's camp saw

the potter riding madly towards them, they were astonished ; when they saw him pull up a tree, they began to be afraid.

" See," they shouted, " he has pulled up a tree ! He must be a demon coming to attack us ! "

They ran back into the camp shouting the news, which soon spread through the army, and grew as it spread. One demon pulling up a tree became ten demons pulling up trees ; ten became a hundred ; a hundred became a thousand, and a thousand many thousands. The whole army was soon in a great fright. With shouts of " They are coming ! They are upon us ! " king, officers, and soldiers fled for their lives, and did not stop till they were back in their own country.

When the potter reached the camp it was empty. His horse stopped ; he untied the knots, and was glad to be once more on his own feet. He walked home, and sent a messenger to tell the king that he would find the enemy gone.

The king could not believe his ears ; he and his courtiers and officers rushed off to the enemy's camp ; they were astonished to find it empty. They rode to the potter's house. The king loaded him with honours and riches, invited him to a great feast, and sent him another splendid horse on which to ride to the palace.

" No more riding for me," said the potter to his wife. He went on foot. The road was lined with thousands of people, who cheered him. They cheered him ten times the more for walking.

" This man is not only brave," they said, " he is modest. Another man would have gone prancing along the road on a charger. This man walks, just like you or me."

The potter was glad to get back home to his pots.

7. THE JACKAL AND THE ALLIGATOR

I

ONE day the jackal was down at the river-side looking for something to eat. What he liked best were the little river crabs ; soon he saw one running into the water. He was after it in an instant, but he was only in time to see it pushing through the roots of the water-plants. Quickly he plunged in his paw.

Snap !

But it was not the little crab that was caught ; it was the jackal. His paw was gripped tight between the jaws of the alligator, who was hiding in the reeds. He felt himself being pulled into the water. That made him think very quickly indeed.

In his most cheerful voice he said :

" Ho, ho ! you clever alligator. So you

thought you had caught me, did you ? Ha, ha !
I hope you like chewing the reed you have in
your mouth. Good-bye ! "

" Well, I never ! " said the alligator. " I
made sure I had him that time."

As soon as he opened his jaws to speak, the
jackal snatched away his paw and said :

" So you let me go, did you ? You clever old
alligator ! " and off he ran, while the alligator
made an angry rush up the bank, snapping his
jaws.

The jackal was so fond of eating crabs that
next day he was once more down at the river ;
but he felt afraid, and dared not begin hunting
till he knew where the alligator lay. So he ran
along the bank saying aloud, as if talking to
himself :

" There can't be any crabs in the water to-day ;
if there were, I should see the bubbles coming up
and going off with a pop. The crabs must have
gone up the bank, and I will go after them."

When the alligator, who lay under the water,
saw the jackal pass, and heard him say he would
go up the bank, he at once began to stir the mud.
That sent hundreds of bubbles to the top, and
they went off with hundreds of pops.

" So there you are, you old dear ! " cried the
jackal. " How sweet of you to let me know !
Bye-bye ! " and he ran off to another part of the
river.

"I will catch him yet," said the alligator, as he rushed up the bank snapping his jaws.

The next day the little jackal did not go to the river. He was too much afraid. He stopped in the jungle and ate wild figs. He did not care as much for them as he did for crabs, but it was better to eat figs than to be eaten oneself.

When the alligator was tired of waiting for the jackal, he set out to look for him in the jungle. He thought the fig tree a likely place to find him, and was not surprised to see him there. He lay hid until the jackal had gone ; then he got together all the figs that had fallen and covered himself over with them. He waited.

When the jackal came again to the fig tree the first thing he saw was a long heap of figs. "Those figs could not get into that heap by themselves," thought he. Then he sniffed the air. "What a queer smell they have. I wonder, now, if there is something under them."

He went a little bit nearer, and said aloud:

"These figs cannot be ripe. Ripe figs roll about a bit as if they were alive. I had better be off to that other tree."

On hearing that, the alligator moved his body very gently from side to side, to make the figs roll about a bit. But the figs rolled off his back, and there he stood looking very foolish.

"How very nice to meet you once more!" said the jackal politely. "Having a little picnic by yourself in the country, I suppose ? So glad you like figs ; they are so much easier to get than jackals. As for me, I like crabs better, and I am off to look for some."

He ran off to the river, knowing that he would have time for his hunting before the alligator could get there.

II

After snapping at the air with his jaws, and lashing the ground with his tail, the alligator hissed : " I will catch that jackal, or die."

In the long grass near the fig tree he noticed the beginning of the narrow path, or track, along which the jackal had come. He went up it, and on reaching the end found himself before a little hole in the side of a hillock. It was the entrance to the jackal's home.

" Very good," said the alligator. " I will now get inside and wait for my little friend to come home. When he does, SNAP !—and that will be the end of him."

When the jackal came back to his hole he stopped short. The entrance to the hole was twice the size it used to be, and the earth above the hole looked as if it had been shaken by an earthquake.

" Dear me," thought the jackal, " what does

this mean ? " He trotted nearer to the hole and said : " Little house, why do you not say good-day to me as you always do when I come back ? Is anything wrong ? "

On hearing that, the alligator, in a voice that he meant to be soft, but which sounded like the squeaking of a cart-wheel, replied :

" All is well, sweet little jackal. Enter, my dear. Come in."

When the jackal heard that voice he trembled with fright. He thought quickly what to do, and said :

" Thank you, my dear little house. What a joy it is to hear your soft and friendly voice. In a moment I will be with you. But first I must get some firewood to cook my supper."

" Do so, my dear ; do so, but be quick," creaked the alligator.

The jackal soon made a heap of dried twigs and grass close to the entrance of his home, while the alligator looked on and smiled. The jackal set fire to the heap, and with his hind feet kicked it into the hole.

The alligator stopped smiling. The crackling flames frightened him ; he drew back as far as he could. It was no use. The wind drove the smoke in and stifled him, and the flames came in and burnt him to a cinder.

As for the jackal, he ran bounding through the jungle, with his tail up, crying :

" I, the jackal, who am small and weak, have killed the alligator, who is large and strong. Ring-a-ding, ring-a-ding, ding-ding-dong ! "

8. THE TIGER AND THE PRIEST

A PRIEST was passing by an iron cage in which a tiger, trapped by the villagers, had been locked up.

" Have pity on me ! " cried the tiger. " Have pity on me, good priest ! Let me out for just a minute—a little minute, so that I can drink. I am dying of thirst. Have pity ! "

" Not I," said the priest. " You would drink and then you would eat me."

" Never would I do such a thing," said the tiger. " Have pity, and let me out, only for one little minute."

The priest had pity, and let out the tiger.

" Now," said the tiger, " I will eat you first, and then drink."

The poor priest, though he trembled with fear, said :

" Very well, but remember I have done you no harm—indeed, I wished to do you good. Do not eat me till you have asked the opinion of six judges. If all say it is right I should die, then kill me."

" Very good," said the tiger. " I will wait a

little till the six have said you must die ; then I will eat you."

They walked on till they came to a fig tree. It was told what the priest had done, and what the tiger wanted to do, and it was asked to give judgment. It said :

" Men take shelter under me, but that does not prevent them from breaking my boughs and pulling off my leaves. Men are vile. Let the tiger eat the priest."

The tiger wanted to eat the man at once ; it seemed to him a waste of time to wait for five more judgments, but at last he agreed to go on.

They met an old camel. On hearing what had happened, he said :

" When I was young I was well treated, well fed. Now I am old, men overload me, starve me, beat me. Men are vile. Let the tiger eat the priest."

" Do you think it worth while going any farther ? " asked the tiger, turning to the priest with an ugly snarl.

" Only two judges out of six have spoken," answered the priest.

" Very well," said the tiger, " let us go on, but let us be quick—very quick."

They came upon an old bullock lying by the roadside, and asked him to judge.

" When I was young," said the bullock, " I served men with all my strength. Now I am old and useless I am left to die by the roadside. Men are vile. Let the tiger eat the priest."

"That makes three," said the tiger, "and I am getting very hungry."

He walked along, snarling savagely, and the man walked after him. They met an eagle. The eagle passed judgment :

"Men shoot at me ; they steal my eggs ; they never leave me in peace. They are all vile. Let the tiger eat the priest."

"Four !" growled the tiger, and he kept roaring with hunger and fury.

They met an alligator. He also passed judgment :

"Whenever I put my nose out of the water men throw things at me and try to kill me. Men are vile. Let the tiger eat the priest."

"Five !" roared the tiger, and he snapped his teeth together, tore at the ground with his paws, and looked at the man with hungry, flaming, yellow eyes.

They went on and met a jackal. When the jackal had heard the case, he sat down with a thoughtful air and said :

"I cannot judge without knowing just what happened. To begin with, I must see the place."

They went back.

"Now, where were you standing, Mr. Priest ?"

"I was standing just here," said the priest.

" Where was the tiger then ? "

" In the cage."

" Where in the cage ? "

" Just here," said the tiger, walking into the cage.

" Yes ; but I must know all.   Which way were you looking ? "

" This way," said the tiger, turning round.

" Was the door open or shut ? "

" Shut and bolted," said the priest.

" Shut and bolt it," said the jackal.

The priest did so.   The jackal then turned on the tiger and said :

" You wicked tiger, when this good priest had pity on you, and let you out, all you thought of was to eat him.   You will stop in this cage. Friend priest, your road lies that way ; mine lies this.   Good-bye."

9. STOP TO THINK

A MAN caught a partridge and was about to kill it, when the bird cried out :

" Man, I can tell you four things you ought to know."

" Oh, indeed," said the man, laughing.   " What are they ? "

" The first is : Keep what you catch."

" You may be sure I will," said the man.

" Here is the second : It is no use crying over spilt milk."

" I have heard that before," said the man.

" The third is : Never believe all you hear."

" Why should I," said the man. " What is the fourth thing ? "

" Ah," said the partridge, " the fourth is the most important, I can only tell you that if I am set free."

The man, without stopping to think, let the bird go. It flew into a tree, and said :

" You do not take much notice of what I tell you. I said : Keep what you catch. Yet you have let me go."

" Why, so I have," said the man, scratching his head. " I did not think what I was doing. Well, never mind ; a partridge is no great loss. Tell me what the fourth thing is."

" The fourth thing is this : In my inside there is a diamond weighing ten pounds. If you had kept what you had caught, you would now be a rich man."

The man fell on the ground, and rolled about weeping and groaning and tearing up the grass.

" You have forgotten the second thing I told you," said the bird: " It is no use crying over spilt milk. Have you also forgotten the third ? "

" What does it matter if I have ? " said the man crossly.

" It may matter a good deal," said the bird.

" Here it is once more : Never believe all you hear."

" Eh, what ? " shouted the man, jumping up and wiping his eyes with the back of his hand. " Do you mean to tell me that you have not got that diamond inside you ? "

" Do you really suppose," said the partridge, " that there is such a thing as a ten-pound diamond, or that there would be room for it in my body, which is no bigger than your fist ? I will give you a piece of advice that is worth more than diamonds. It is : Stop to think."

10. THE RATS AND THE BARS OF IRON ; or, TIT FOR TAT

A MERCHANT was about to go on a long journey into foreign lands. He had some bars of iron which he did not want to take with him, so he went to one of his neighbours, who had in his garden an empty shed. He asked him to keep the bars locked up in the shed till his return. The neighbour agreed to do so on payment of a sum.

When the merchant had been away some time the neighbour said to himself : " That man will never come back. I may as well sell his iron bars, and put the money into my pocket."

One day the merchant did come back. When he asked for his iron, the neighbour said :

" Your iron ? Well, I am very sorry to have to tell you that your iron is gone."

" Gone ! " cried the merchant.

" Yes," said the neighbour. " Come and see."

He took him to the shed. It was empty. There was nothing to be seen in it but a few rats. The merchant was astonished.

" How on earth was my iron stolen ? " asked he.

The neighbour gave the first answer that came into his head.

" Those rats must have eaten it."

The merchant guessed what had really happened, but he pretended to believe the story.

" What a foolish fellow ! " said the neighbour as he watched the merchant going slowly and sadly away.

A few days later the merchant met in the road the son of the neighbour, a dear little boy about three. He gave the dear little boy some sweets, and took him for a walk.

They went into a big wood, and as they went the merchant told wonderful stories of the fairies. Then, in the very heart of the wood, they found a lovely little house made of logs. In it were a table and two chairs. On the table were all the cakes you can think of, and also ices and lemonade.

The dear little boy was quite sure that the hut had been built, and the food put there, by the fairies. The merchant knew better, but he only smiled.

They sat down, and the little boy ate every kind of cake on the table, and with every cake he took some ice, and drank some lemonade. He was beginning all over again when he found that he could hardly keep his eyes open. He lay down on a bed of bracken and moss, which he was also sure the fairies had put there. In a few minutes he was fast asleep.

After closing the door carefully, the merchant went back. About an hour later he met his neighbour running along the road, weeping and tearing his hair, and crying that his son was lost.

" Have you seen my boy ? " he shouted, as soon as he saw the merchant.

" Yes," said the merchant, " I saw him a few hours ago."

" Where ? " cried the neighbour.

" I saw him," replied the merchant, " in the claws of a sparrow. It was flying away with him into the woods."

" What ! " screamed the neighbour. " What do you mean by talking such rubbish ? As if a sparrow could carry off my boy."

" Why not ? " answered the merchant quietly. " If rats can eat iron, surely a sparrow can carry a boy."

The neighbour guessed easily what the merchant meant. He gave up, there and then, the money he had got for the iron, after which the

two men went into the wood.   There, in the hut,
they found the dear little boy still fast asleep.

11. THE MONKEYS WATER THE
FLOWER-BEDS

ONE fine day a gardener wanted to go to the
play.

" If I go, who is to water the flower-beds ? "

He could think of no one.   Suddenly he remembered that some monkeys lived in the trees
at the bottom of the garden.   He went and
called them.   They came swinging from branch
to branch, and sprang to the ground in front of
him ; they sat down round him.

" Monkeys," said he, " I have been a good
friend to you.   I have let you take nuts and fruit
in the garden.   Now I am going to ask you to
do something for me."

" Say what it is," cried the monkeys ; " it
shall be done."

The gardener told them that he wanted them
to water the garden while he was away.   He
gave them a watering-can, showed them how to
let down the bucket into the well, and went off.

The leader of the monkeys called the rest
together, and spoke thus :

" Monkeys, our friend the gardener has done
us the honour to ask a service of us.   We must

do it in an orderly and careful manner. The first thing is to look at the well."

They peered down the well, and thinking there was no more water than what they saw, they decided that they must make the water go as far as possible.

" The best way is to give most water to the plants that most need it," said the leader.

" How are we to know which plants most need it ? " asked one of them.

The leader thought a while, then he answered :

" The plants with the longest roots will want the most water ; those with short roots, the least."

That seemed so clear that it was agreed to at once.

" The only way," continued the leader, " to know which plants have long roots, and which short is, of course, to pull them up and look at the roots."

That also seemed so clear that it was at once agreed to.

They got to work. One set were told to draw up the water ; they at once began to squabble, for each wanted to turn the handle that let the bucket down. They pushed, and clawed, and bit. The struggle ended in a monkey falling into the well. He was pulled up in the bucket, half drowned. The leader then decided to work the bucket himself.

Another set carried the watering-can to the
plants. As each wanted to hold the handle, and
fought to do so, most of the water was spilt on
the way. The greater part of what was left was
used to sprinkle other monkeys, this being better
fun than watering the plants, which got very
little.

A third set pulled up the plants and set them
in rows, with the roots spread out so that the
length of the roots could be seen. As it was more
trouble to put the plants back than to pull them
up, they were left lying.

The monkeys were still hard at it when the
gardener returned.

As soon as he saw what they had done, he
shouted :

" Oh, you foolish animals, what *have* you been
doing ? "

He raised his stick, and was about to beat the
monkeys in his rage, when a quiet voice said
behind him :

" It is you who are foolish—not the monkeys."

It was the voice of his master, the owner of the
garden.

12. THE CRANE AND THE CRAB

A CRANE found a pool of water in which were a
number of fish. The pool was small and hot ;
the fish did not like it, and swam about saying

so loudly. The crane heard them, and that gave him an idea.

He went to the pool, and said he knew of a big, cool pool not far off to which he would carry them, if they liked.

" We do not believe you," said the fish; " you want to catch and eat us. We know you. Go away."

" It is true," said the crane, " that I have eaten a fish or two in my time, but to show you that I mean well I make this offer. If one of you has the pluck to let himself be carried to the big pool, I will take him in my beak and bring him back to tell you what the pool is like."

After much talking among themselves, one of the fish, bolder than the others, made up his mind to go. The crane carried him gently to a fine large pool, let him swim about in it, and then carried him back.

What the fish said about the big pool made all the other fish want to go at once. They rolled and flapped out of the water, on to the bank, all round the crane's feet, screaming, " Me first! Me first!" The crane found it hard not to swallow some of them there and then. He said:

" The first must be the one who took the risk of going in my beak to the pool. He deserves to be the first."

All the fish agreed to that. So the crane

carried the same fish in the direction of the big pool, but he did not go there. At the first suitable spot he came down to ground and swallowed the fish.

Whenever he felt hungry he took another fish to the same spot. After a time there were none left. The crane looked down into the pool hoping to see one; all he saw was a big crab. He offered to carry him, but the crab had more sense than the fish. He said:

" If you carry me in your beak you may perhaps forget me, and let me drop."

" Not I," said the crane. " Why should I ? "

" You wouldn't do it on purpose, I know," said the crab; " but I am so timid, I do not like to risk it."

" How else can I carry you, except in my beak ? " asked the crane.

" It might do if I got hold of your neck with one of my claws."

The crane, who was feeling very hungry, agreed. The crab gripped his neck, and off they went through the air. Soon the crab noticed that they were going down to a place all covered with fish bones.

" Where are we going, dear crane ? " asked he.

" We are going to my dining-room, and you are the dinner, dear crab."

" Am I ? " asked the crab, as he gave the crane's neck a little nip with the strong claws.

That nip made the crane feel what a mistake he had made. Suppose the crab were to nip with all his strength, what would happen ? The more the crane thought about it, the less he liked it. He ended by promising to take the crab to the big pool, and came down close to its edge. He hoped that as soon as the crab let go his neck he would be able to kill him before he reached the water.

The crab knew quite well what the crane was thinking. As soon as the bird's feet touched the ground the strong claws cut like a pair of scissors clean through the neck. That was the end of the crane.

13. THE WEASEL, THE RABBIT, AND THE CAT

A YOUNG rabbit came back to its hole to find it taken by a weasel.

" Come out of my hole at once," said the rabbit. " If you do not, I will call all the rats in the place, and set them on to you."

" Why should I go ? " asked the weasel. ' What right have you to this hole more than any one else ? "

" It was left me by my father," replied the rabbit, " and it was left him by his father. What better right could one have ? "

" Yes ; but who had it before your grandfather stole it ? "

" Stole it ! What right have you to talk about stealing ? " screamed the rabbit.

They went on disputing. In the end they decided to put the matter before a very learned cat, who lived in a wood near by.

" My children," said the cat, " come a little nearer. I am old and deaf, very deaf. Come still a little closer. Ah ! "

The cat shot out his paws and caught both. He settled their dispute by making a meal of them.

14. ONCE A CAT, ALWAYS A CAT

FOUR animals lived in an old tree, each in his hole. There was the cat near the bottom, and not far from him the rat. Higher up the owl had his home, and a little farther down the weasel. They were all well known to the man who owned the tree ; he knew them to be rascals, and did his best to get rid of them.

One day the cat was caught in one of his nets. As the cat lay there, struggling wildly to get free, the rat passed and was only too pleased to see his deadly enemy a prisoner. The cat stopped struggling, and said :

" Dear friend, no one knows better than I do your goodness and kindness. That is why I have never done you any harm. I have loved you as I have loved my own eyes ; and now I count on you to free me from the net that hateful man has set here to catch me, as well as you."

" What will you give me if I set you free ? " asked the rat.

" I will give you my friendship," said the cat. " I will protect you against your enemies, and I will begin by killing the worst of them—the owl and the weasel."

The rat laughed. " Do you really think, you wretch, that I am going to set you free ? I am not so foolish."

He went off to his hole, but on the way he met the weasel, and on turning aside he nearly ran into the owl. So he fled back, and finding himself followed by both the weasel and the owl, bit through the net and freed the cat. He knew that as soon as the others saw the cat coming they would be frightened away.

At the same moment the man arrived, and all four rascals fled to their holes.

Some days afterwards the rat met the cat, and took good care to keep out of his reach. The cat looked hurt by this treatment, and said :

" Ah, my dear friend, why do you treat me like an enemy ? Did you not save my life ? Come and let me embrace you. Do you think I could ever forget the service you have done me ? "

" Do you think," said the rat, " that I could

ever forget who you are ? Once a cat, always a cat ! "

The rat sprang away, and only just in time; the cat's paw struck down upon the very spot where he had been.

15. THE THREE ROGUES

A PRIEST bought a lamb and was carrying it home on his shoulder. He was seen by three rogues, who made a plan to rob him of the lamb without seeming to do so.

They sat down, each by the roadside at some distance one from the other, and waited for the priest to pass.

The first rogue saluted him as he went by, and asked :

" Why, O priest, do you carry a dog on your shoulder ? "

" It is not a dog," answered the priest, " it is a lamb."

The second rogue saluted him as he passed, and asked him :

" Why, O priest, do you carry a dog on your shoulder ? "

The priest put the lamb down and looked at it again and again, then he said :

" A dog ? What on earth do you mean ? Surely you know a lamb when you see one ? "

He put the lamb back on his shoulder and walked on, but he could not help feeling that he might be mistaken about what he was carrying. Then he thought, " It must be a lamb," then again he began to doubt. While he was doubting, he came to the third rogue, who saluted him and said :

" Why, O priest, do you carry a dog on your shoulder ? "

That settled the matter. The priest now felt sure that there must be something wrong with his eyes, and that people thought him very foolish to go about with a dog on his shoulder. So he threw his load into the ditch, and went his way wondering how he was to be cured.

The three rogues caught the lamb, cooked it, and had a feast.

16. THE SHEPHERD AND THE KING

ONE day a king was passing over a grassy plain. It was covered with flocks of sheep. They were his own sheep, and he noticed how fine they were. He was told that they brought him much money each year, so he sent for the shepherd and said to him :

" You are so good a master of sheep that I will make you a master of men. You shall be the chief judge in my kingdom."

The shepherd became a judge, and punished all those who did wrong.

Though he did not know it, the judge had many enemies. Some hated him because they did not think a common shepherd ought to be made a judge; others hated him because he refused the money they offered him to let them off being punished. All these people tried to set the king against him. They said that he thought of nothing but riches, and that his house was full of costly furniture.

The king went to his house; he found in it the furniture one sees in a cottage.

"That," said his enemies, "is just pretence. His riches are all in a huge chest with ten steel locks. It is full of gold and silver and gems."

The king went again to the shepherd's house and ordered him to open the chest before them all. It was not difficult, for there was only one lock, and it was broken.

When the shepherd lifted the lid everybody looked into the chest. What did they see? All they saw was a shepherd's dress and his stick.

The judge let fall the clothes he was wearing. Before them all he took out the shepherd's dress and put it on; then he took the stick.

"These clothes and this stick," said he, "are all I had when I came here. They are all I have now that I go."

He went to his flock and did not return.

17. THE SQUIRREL, THE OWL, AND THE MOLE

THE squirrel, the owl, and the mole lived together. One day they wished to go to the butcher's shop to buy some meat. As they were in a great hurry, they harnessed two tigers to a cart ; in front of the tigers they put two leopards ; in front of the leopards two jackals ; and in front of the jackals two hares. Then they started.

The hares ran as fast as they could because they did not want to be caught and eaten by the jackals ; the jackals ran as fast as they could because they wanted to eat the hares and did not want to be caught and eaten by the leopards ; the leopards did the same because they wanted to eat the jackals and did not want to be caught and eaten by the tigers ; and the tigers ran their best to catch and eat the leopards.

The cart went jolting and bounding through the forest, sometimes on one wheel, sometimes on both, as no cart had ever jolted and bounded before.

The squirrel was driver, and sat in front cracking his whip and saying, "Kch! Kch! Kch!" That is why squirrels say "Kch! Kch! Kch!" to this day.

The owl was in the middle of the cart, and kept looking to see that the wheels did not come off.

He stood with his feet wide apart to steady himself, and he kept turning his head quickly from side to side, so as to watch both wheels. So quickly did he turn his head that his eyes nearly started out. That is why owls came to have such staring eyes.

The mole lay in the back of the cart, looking at the owl jerking his head from side to side, and he laughed and he laughed till *his* eyes went right into his head. That is why moles are so blind.

When the butcher saw a cart drawn by leopards and tigers coming out of the forest, he at once put up his shutters. No more was seen or heard of him that day.

The squirrel pulled up, and the three friends considered what to do. While they were considering, the hares were gobbled up by the jackals, the jackals by the leopards, the leopards by the tigers. The two tigers alone remained. As they had each eaten a leopard, a jackal, and a hare, they were quite unable to move a step.

Seeing that there was no getting back, the squirrel said :

" These tigers will have to do for our lunch."

He cut them up with a carving knife ; the mole made a fire ; the owl did the cooking.

When the meal was ready, the squirrel rang the dinner-bell, " Kch ! Kch ! Kch ! " and they all sat down to roast tiger-leopard-jackal-hare. They went on eating till nothing was left but bones and skins.

"This only shows," said the owl, blinking at his friends, "that enough is as good as a feast."

"What you mean," said the owl, in a sleepy voice, "is that a feast is as good as enough."

"Kch! Kch! Kch!" said the squirrel. "What you really mean is that a feast is much better than enough."

The owl opened his beak to argue, but saw that the other two were fast asleep. He fell asleep himself.

18. THE TOWN MOUSE AND THE COUNTRY MOUSE

Town Mouse. Good-day! What brings you up to town, and how are you?

Country Mouse. Oh, not very well. My appetite has gone; I have come up to see a doctor.

Town Mouse. A doctor! What is the use of a doctor? Just you come with me; I will show you a meal that will give you an appetite as soon as you see it. Come along.

Country Mouse. All right, but I am afraid I shall not be able to eat. . . .

Town Mouse. You wait and see. Come along . . . come along.

The two mice entered a house ; soon they were on a table covered with what was left of a big meal.

Town Mouse. Here you are ! Here is everything you can want : cheese, wax candles, cake, ham sandwiches, apples. . . . I am going to begin with wax candle. . . .

The country mouse did not answer ; his head was already buried in the cheese.

There was a noise ; the door was being quietly pushed open. The mice did not wait to see who was coming in. With one bound they were off the table and running to their hole. They reached it only just in time. Tabby's paw missed the country mouse by no more than an inch.

After a time the mice came out again and looked round.

Town Mouse. She has gone. We can finish our meal.

For answer the country mouse took up his hat.

Town Mouse. What ! Are you going ? Are you afraid of that old cat ?

Country Mouse. Yes, I am.

Town Mouse. What nonsense ! Remember that he who risks nothing gains nothing.

Country Mouse. That is so, but when the risk means death, and the gain is only a meal, the risk is not worth taking. I bid you good-day.

The country mouse put on his hat, took his

The mice did not wait to see who was coming in.

stick, and walked out, saying to himself, "What a stupid fellow!"

The town mouse climbed up again on to the table, saying as he did so: "What a stupid fellow! As for me, I will finish my meal."

" No, you will not ; but I am going to begin mine," said Tabby, as she sprang out from behind a bowl of flowers and smacked a paw down upon the back of the town mouse.*

19. THE HERON

A HERON, who was hungry, came to a pool in which there were some fine fish.

" Nice fish, but not big enough," said he, and he walked on.

Soon he came to another pool. There were fish here also, but not so big as those in the first pool.

" Not worth eating ! " said the heron, and he walked on.

He found no fish in the next pool ; there were only a few frogs sitting on a lily leaf.

" Eat frogs ? Not I ! " said the heron, and again he walked on.

In the next pool were a few tadpoles.

" Tadpoles ! " said the heron. " Am I to fill my beak with wretched baby frogs ? I would just as soon eat snails or slugs."

He walked on, and after some time came to the source of the stream. It was just a little trickle of water that rose up out of the ground. There

* This fable grew out of the Indian fable of the Thin Cat and the Fat Cat (p. 7).

the heron saw nothing to eat—not a fish, and neither frogs nor tadpoles. As he was turning to go, he noticed, crawling up the side of a stone, a horrid black slug.

" Ugh ! " said the heron.

All the same, he ate the horrid black slug.

20. THE FOX GIVES AND LEARNS A LESSON

I

ONE day a fox saw a crow on the branch of a tree. The crow had something in its beak.

" Hallo ! What has he got there ? " said the fox to himself.

On going closer, he saw that the thing was a bit of cheese.

" Ho, ho ! " said he. " I should like that cheese. I wonder, now, if I could make him drop it."

He sat down under the tree, and, looking up, he said :

" Good-day, Mr. Crow. How splendid you are this morning with the sun shining on those beautiful black feathers of yours. It does one good just to sit and look at you."

The crow was much pleased, and was about to say so, when he remembered, just in time, that

The crow had something in its beak.

he had the cheese in his beak. He nodded
instead.

" Oh, bother the bird ! " said the fox to himself. Then, smiling as if he were delighted, he
tried again.

" You know, Mr. Crow, I heard it said the other day that your voice is as beautiful as your feathers. I do not know whether that is true or not, for I have never heard you sing. If it is true, you must be a wonderful bird—a most wonderful bird."

On hearing that, the crow opened his beak wide and cawed and croaked his very loudest.

"Caw! Kraa! Caw! Kraa! Kraa! Caw!"

Down fell the cheese. It fell into the mouth of the fox, who gobbled it up in a second, and in another second was out of sight.

The crow stopped his cawing and croaking; he felt very silly. He declared he would never again listen to flattery.

II

Next day the fox was passing the same tree. Looking up, he saw a barn-cock on the very branch on which the crow had sat. The barn-cock was big and plump. The fox's mouth began to water at the sight of him.

" I must make him come down," said he to himself. He put on a friendly air and began :

" Good-day, brother. I have news for you, good news—most wonderful news. . . ."

" Indeed," said the barn-cock politely.

" Yes, and I bring it straight from the court of

King Lion himself. He and the other chief
animals have made a law that all of us must live
in peace from to-day. No bird or beast is to be
eaten for food   The lion is to be friends with the
ox, the wolf to be friends with the lamb, the fox
with the barn fowl, and so with every creature.
Just try and think what that means."

" I am trying to think," said the barn-cock.

" I will tell you one thing that it means,"
continued the fox. " It means that you and I
can go about and play, and have a fine time
together ; so come down."

The barn-cock made as if to fly down, then
paused. He stretched up his neck, and looked
over the hedge into the next field.

" Why, that is the farm dog I see. He will be
here in a few seconds. If you will wait, we can
then, all three, have a fine time together."

" I am afraid I cannot wait even a few seconds,"
said the fox. " I must carry the good news to
others."

Then off he ran.

The barn-cock laughed to himself. He was
very pleased to have tricked a trickster.

21. THE FOX AND THE STORKS

I

ONE morning a stork was busy looking for food.
He met the fox, and asked him if he had seen
anything good to eat.

"The only thing good to eat that I know of,"
answered the fox, "is my own breakfast. It is
waiting for me in my hole there. I can smell it.
What a lovely smell it has!" And he sniffed
the air.

The stork also smelt it; never had anything
smelt so nice: it made him feel all the hungrier.

"Perhaps you would like to have some of my
breakfast?" said the fox politely.

For a moment the stork could not answer: he
was too much astonished. Never before had he
known the fox do a good deed. When he found
his breath, he said:

"You are very kind. I shall be only too happy
to accept your invitation."

"Good!" said the fox. "Will you just wait
a second or two, and I will bring the meal out."

Presently out he came with a dish of nice hot
soup, which he placed on the ground.

"Set to, Mr. Stork, set to. Take just as much
as you like."

The stork did set to; but all he got was about

six drops. The fox had served the soup in a flat dish. The narrow tip of the stork's beak could scoop up only a little at a time. The fox's tongue lapped it up in a twinkling.

" That was good ! " said the fox, as he licked up the last drop. Then, with a spiteful grin on his face, he vanished into his hole.

II

The stork went away feeling as hungry as ever, for six drops is not much of a meal. He made up his mind to be even with that fox. He talked things over with Mrs. Stork. A few days later, this is what happened.

The fox was passing near where the storks lived, when there came to his nose a lovely smell of cooking breakfast. On turning to look, he saw only Mrs. Stork at home.

" Good ! " said he, " I will make her give me some of that breakfast."

Going up to Mrs. Stork, he said " Good-day," and added, " One has only to sniff the air to be sure that you are a wonderful cook, Mrs. Stork."

Mrs. Stork pretended to be very pleased, and bowed.

The fox went on to say :

" What a lucky bird Mr. Stork must be to have such a cook for a wife, and so beautiful, too :

such long and graceful legs, such a straight, long beak, and such soft, fine feathers.''

Mrs. Stork pretended to be more pleased than ever, and asked the fox if he would care to taste what she was cooking.

" It is chicken,'' she added.

Now there was nothing in the world the fox liked more than chicken : he was only too pleased to say " Yes.''

Mrs. Stork brought out the chicken in a pot, and begged the fox to help himself. The fox did not wait to be asked twice ; he sprang to the pot and thrust his muzzle into it. Now the pot was so made that he could reach the chicken only with the very tip of his tongue : he could just taste how nice it was, but he could not pick up a morsel. In a fury he then tried to break the pot by pushing hard into it with his muzzle.

While the fox was doing this, he heard, close behind him, the voice of Mr. Stork, who had been hiding near by all the time. The voice said :

" Set to, Mr. Fox, set to. Take just as much as you like.''

The fox in a fright tried to pull his muzzle out of the pot, but he had pushed it in too hard : it was fixed fast.

There he stood looking very foolish, with the pot on his nose. The two storks clattered their bills with laughter. The fox would gladly have bitten them if his jaws had been free. All he

could do was to utter a snarl which sounded very
hollow in the pot. That made the storks laugh
more. The fox filled the pot with another hollow
snarl, and sprang away with his tail between his
legs. He did not stop till he was out of hearing
of that horrid laughter.

Then, seeing a rock, he banged the pot against
it till it broke. Inside it was enough chicken
flesh to cover a penny, also the feet and the beak,
and some feathers.

22. THE HARE AND THE TORTOISE

THE tortoise has a heavy body and short legs ;
he can go only at a slow pace. The hare can go
as quickly as the wind. Yet, once upon a time,
the tortoise and the hare had a race, and it was
the tortoise that won.

It came about in this way.

One day a young hare, who was very fond of
talking about himself, boasted of his speed to an
old tortoise.

" Do you see," said he, " that hill over there ?
It is very far away ; yet in half a minute from
now I could be on the top of it."

The tortoise looked at him and said :

" It is true you run very fast, but for all that
I, the slow tortoise, now challenge you to race
me to the top of that same hill."

The hare was so astonished that he could hardly believe his ears.

"Would you mind saying that again?" he asked.

The tortoise said it again.

"What!" screamed the hare. "You, the slow old tortoise have a race with me, the hare! Well, may the next dog catch me if ever I heard anything so silly." Then he rolled on to his back with his feet in the air, and laughed, and laughed, and laughed till his sides ached.

When the hare stopped laughing, he said:

"Would you mind saying that again?"

"When shall we start?"

"Now," said the tortoise; "and the one who is the first to touch that big tree on the hill wins."

"Very well," said the hare. "Go ahead."

The tortoise went ahead at his usual pace. The hare did not start. He made a huge leap into the air just to show how springy he was, and then lay down to sleep in the middle of a large tuft of grass. He knew he had plenty of time to beat the tortoise.

The old tortoise walked steadily on beneath the baking sun ; he was terribly hot, he felt very thirsty, and his legs ached beneath his heavy body ; but he never stopped. Slowly, bit by bit, without looking to right or left, he drew near to the top of the hill. So slowly did he go that he would still have been beaten if the hare had started in time.

The hare, when he woke up, spent such a long time in stretching himself, in cleaning and smoothing his fur, and in polishing his whiskers, that he did not start till the tortoise was right on top of the hill close to the tree. Then at last away he went off. And he did go ! He made great bounds, and ran so quickly that he seemed hardly to touch the ground. In a minute he was on the top of the hill.

It was too late. The tortoise was already there, touching the tree.

23. COUNTING THE CHICKENS BEFORE THEY ARE HATCHED

A COUNTRY maid was walking along with a can of milk on her head. She was going to sell the milk, and was thinking of what she would do with the money.

" With the money," said she, " I will buy some more eggs ; I shall then have, in all, about three

Down fell the can.

hundred. Some of them may become addled, others may be eaten by rats, but in any case I can safely count on two hundred and fifty being hatched. The chickens will be ready for the market just at the time when poultry fetches a good price. By Christmas I shall have money to spare for a new frock—a green frock. Yes, pale green is the colour that suits me. When I go to the dances in that frock the men will just crowd round me. I shall refuse them all, and I shall refuse them with a toss of my head—just like this. . . ."

She tossed her head. Down fell the can : out poured the milk into the ditch. . . .

Good-bye eggs, chicks, and new frock.

24. THE WOLF AND THE DOG

A WOLF and a dog met in the moonlight. The wolf was thin and hungry, the dog stout and well fed.

The wolf would gladly have torn the dog into little bits, but that meant a fight ; and the wolf was not sure of winning. So he saluted the dog, and was very polite.

" How well you look," he said ; " how fat, how sleek, and here am I half starved and miserable, though I work hard for my living night and day."

" Well, it is your own fault," said the dog. " If you want to be well fed and happy like me, you have only to do as I do."

" What is that ? " asked the wolf.

" Nothing much," answered the dog. " You must guard the master's house, chase away beggars, and be polite to the family."

" Is that all ? " asked the wolf.

" That is all," said the dog. " In return you get plenty of food, plenty of sleep, plenty of fun."

" Splendid," said the wolf. " That will just suit me."

" All right. Come along," said the dog.

As they went on together, the wolf noticed a bare spot on the dog's neck.

" What is that bare spot on your neck ? " asked he.

" Oh, nothing," said the dog.

" But what made it ? " asked the wolf, still curious.

" Probably the collar to which my chain is fastened."

" Chain ! " cried the wolf. " Do you mean to tell me you are not free to run when and where you please ? "

" Sometimes I am chained in the day-time, but that is a small matter. . . ."

" A small matter ? " cried the wolf. " It is anything but a small matter to lose one's freedom. I would much rather starve. A chain ! Not for me ! Good-bye ! "

25. THE GRASSHOPPER AND THE ANT

DURING the summer the ant laid up a store of food for the winter. The grasshopper was less prudent. He laid up nothing, so that when winter came he found himself starving.

One frosty day he could not bear his hunger any longer ; he went begging to the door of the ant.

" Please give me something to keep me alive till the spring," said he ; " I will repay you then in full and more."

" Why," asked the ant, " did you not lay up a store during the summer ? "

" I was busy singing to all who cared to listen."

" You sang all the summer, did you ? Well, you can dance all the winter."

26. THE GOLDEN AXE

A woodman was cutting down a tree on the bank of a river. His axe slipped from his hand and fell into deep water. It was the only axe he had ; without it he could not make a living. He sat down and cried.

Suddenly before him there stood a river god. On hearing the cause of the woodman's trouble, the god dived into the water and brought up a golden axe.

" Is this yours ? " he asked.

" No," said the man.

Again the god dived and brought up a silver axe.

" Is this yours ? "

" No."

So again the god dived, and this time he brought up the lost axe.

" That is mine," said the woodman, glad to have his own back again.

The god told him to keep both the gold axe and the silver one.

The woodman went off with his three axes and told his friends all that had happened. One of them, also a woodman, thought he would try his luck at the same place. So he let fall his axe into the water. Then he sat down and pretended to cry.

Suddenly the god stood before him, and, on hearing the cause of his trouble, dived into the water. He came up with a shining golden axe in his hand.

" Is this yours ? " asked he.

" Yes, that is it," said the man eagerly, stretching out his hand.

There and then the god vanished, and with him the golden axe. The man lost also his own axe.

27. THE WOLF AND THE STORK

A WOLF, who was in the habit of gulping down his food, found himself with a bone stuck in his throat. He beckoned with his paw to a passing stork, and opening his jaw pointed down it. The stork understood. It put in its long beak and pulled out the bone.

" Well, I *am* glad to be rid of that bone," said the wolf, looking very pleased.

" What about the money for my services ? " asked the stork.

The wolf looked pleased no longer.

" Money for your services ? " he snarled. " Are you joking ? Isn't it enough that you put your head into a wolf's mouth without having it bitten off ? Away with you, ungrateful fowl, and see that you never again come within reach of my jaws."

28. THE WOLF AND THE LAMB

" How dare you dirty my drinking-water, you wretch ! " snarled the wolf.

" I am not dirtying your water," answered the lamb. " How can I dirty it ? The stream flows down from you to me."

" What do I care whether it flows down or whether it flows up ! " growled the wolf. " All I know is that last year you went everywhere saying horrid things about me."

" How could I ? " answered the lamb, trembling ; " I was not even born."

" Well, if it was not you," said the wolf savagely, " it was your father, or your mother, or one of

your relatives. What does it matter? I have had enough of you all, you and your shepherds and your dogs! You deserve to die, and you shall.''

Without another word he tore the poor lamb to pieces.

29. THE LION AND THE MOUSE

A LION, who was having a nap, felt something run over his nose. He opened his eyes and clapped his paw on a mouse.

" How dare you run over my nose ? " he snarled.

The mouse, almost frightened to death, replied that he had done it without thinking. He begged His Majesty not to put his mighty paw to the trouble of crushing such a wretched little creature as a mouse.

The lion, amused at his answer, let him go ; and the mouse was only too glad to escape so easily. Before going, he turned and said he hoped some day to be able to do the lion a good turn. That amused the lion still more ; he laughed, for he could not imagine how a tiny creature like a mouse could help the great king of beasts.

A few days later the lion was caught in a net. He struggled and struck and bit, but it was all of no use ; the net held him fast.

The mouse heard the angry roaring of the lion, and ran to the spot. He jumped up and down in front of the lion's face until he was noticed ; then he screamed to him to keep quite still while he set him free.

The lion looked at him with astonishment, but he soon understood. The mouse's sharp, cutting teeth bit quickly through one cord after another. In a few minutes the lion had only to crawl out.

30. LOOK BEFORE YOU LEAP

A FOX fell into a well. There was not enough water to drown him, but as he had no wish to be found there by the villagers, he was anxious to get out quickly. While he was wondering what to do, he looked up, and there, at the top of the well, saw a goat looking down.

" Good-day," said the fox.

" Good-day," said the goat. " What are you doing down there ? "

" I am drinking this water ; it is so good I cannot drink enough. Just you come and try it."

The goat, without stopping to think, leapt down, for he was thirsty. When he had finished drinking he looked about him and said :

" How do we get out ? "

" That is quite easy," answered the fox. " You stand up on your hind feet, and put your front feet against the side of the well ; I will scramble up your back and jump out ; then, of course, I will pull you out."

" What a splendid idea ! " said the goat. " I should never have thought of it myself."

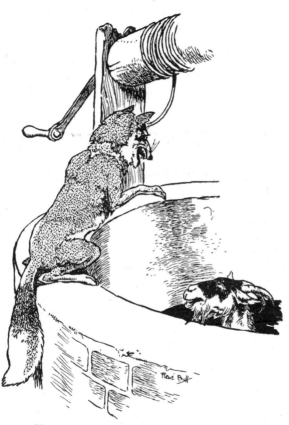

"You can stop where you are, my friend."

In a few seconds the fox was outside the well. Then he turned and, looking down at the goat with a spiteful grin, said :

" You can stop where you are, my friend ; if you had as much sense in your head as you have beard on your chin, you would have looked before you leapt."

31. KING LOG AND KING STORK

THE frogs were tired of trying to rule themselves, so they begged their god to give them a king.

" Very well," he said, " I will send you a king."

Next moment the king fell into the pool with a great splash. The frogs were frightened out of their wits ; they hid in the mud, and in any hole they could find.

In time one frog, bolder than the others, dared to come out of his hiding-place and look. What he saw was a log. Down he dived to tell the others. It was not long before they were all looking at the log, and wondering what it would do. It did nothing.

The log went on doing nothing. The frogs swam up to it and around it. Some dared to jump on to it in order to sun themselves. Soon all were sunning themselves and talking about King Log as they sat on his back. They did not think much of him. They said so. They wanted a king who did things ; so they begged their god to send them a king—a real king who *did* things.

" You are never satisfied," said the god. " You are always wanting something new. Now this is the last time I shall listen to your complaints. You shall have a new king, and he will certainly do things."

The new king stepped into the pool. It was a stork. He began his reign by snapping up and gulping down one frog after another.

It was not long before the frogs were complaining of King Stork and his way of doing things, but the god turned a deaf ear to them.

32. THE SICK LION

A LION, falling ill, was unable to leave his den to hunt for food. He sent round a message to the other animals, inviting them to visit him. He wanted, said he, a few friends to help him to pass the time.

Most of the animals went to see the lion, some out of kindness, others because they thought it rather fine to visit the King of Beasts. One animal did not go. That was the fox. On being sent for, he stood outside the den, and asked His Majesty how he felt.

" Ah, my dear friend," said the lion, " so it is you ! Why have you not been before, and why

do you stand there outside ?   Come in, come in
and sit with the poor old lion, for he has only a
few days to live."

" I should have been most happy to enter and
sit with Your Majesty a while," said the fox
coldly, " if I had not noticed one thing."

" Oh, indeed," said the lion, " and pray what
is that ? "

" I have noticed," answered the fox, " that all
the footprints here point towards your den ; not
one points outwards ! "

33. SOUR GRAPES

THERE was once a fox who was out looking for a
meal.   He came to a vine, on which hung beautiful bunches of grapes.

" What lovely ripe grapes ! " said the fox to
himself.   " I'll just jump up and get a bunch."

He jumped once, twice, three times, four times ;
and each time he made a snap with his jaws at
the nearest bunch.   He never jumped so high in
his life, but it was all of no use.

He felt very cross, and though he wanted the
grapes all the more because he could not get
them, he pretended he did not want them.

" Those grapes," he cried, " are no good ; they
are sour ! "

"What lovely ripe grapes!"

34. THE FROGS AND THE OX

SOME frogs were admiring the size and strength of an ox.

" It would be fine to be big like that ! " said a little frog.

" I could be just as big if I tried," said a big one.

The others laughed at him.

" Well, just you watch and see ! " said he. Then he began to blow himself out till he was twice his size.

" What about that ? " he asked.

" Why, you are not nearly as big."

The frog tried again ; he puffed and puffed till his skin was stretched as tight as a drum.

" What about that ? " he asked.

" Nowhere near," cried the others.

He tried again. He swelled and stretched, and stretched and swelled till, all at once, he burst his skin. And that was the end of him.

35. THE EAGLE AND THE BEETLE

A RABBIT, hunted by an eagle, was running to its hole. On the way it passed the hole of its friend, the beetle. Almost dead with fright, it threw itself down. At the same moment the eagle came down ; she was about to snatch up the rabbit, when the beetle addressed her with these words :

"Great Queen of Birds, it is easy for you to carry off this poor trembling beast. I cannot stop you ; I can only beg you to spare his life. He is my friend.   Spare his life, or kill us both."

The eagle did not trouble to reply.   She swept the beetle aside with her wing, and flew off with the rabbit in her strong claws.

The beetle picked himself up and, opening his wings, went straight to the eagle's nest.   He hid himself till she was away, then he pushed all the eggs out of her nest ; they fell to the ground and were broken.

When the eagle returned to find her eggs broken, she filled the sky with cries of rage and grief, but her cries were useless.   She could have no more eggs for a year.

Next spring she built her nest on a higher spot, hoping it would be safer, for she thought her eggs had been broken by a shepherd.

Once more the beetle came, waited till the eagle was away, and once more sent every egg to the ground in pieces.

This time the cries of the eagle were terrible to hear. The beetle began to think that his friend the rabbit had been revenged, but he was not yet quite satisfied.

When the next spring came, the eagle went to

the god Jupiter and asked him to let her leave her eggs in his lap. She thought that there they would be safe. Jupiter allowed her to do so.

While he sat on his high mountain, with the eggs in his lap, the beetle arrived. The beetle dared not push the eggs off the lap. What he did was to make a pellet of dirt and let it drop on to Jupiter's knees. The god at once shook it off, and, without thinking, shook off the eggs at the same time. They fell and were broken.

The eagle nearly died of grief and rage. The beetle, thinking he had done enough, went to Jupiter and told him all.

Jupiter agreed that the eagle had done wrong, but thought she had been punished enough. As he could not change her and the beetle into friends, he changed the time when the eagle lays her eggs. He chose the time when beetles shut themselves up in their holes to sleep day and night.

36. THE WISE LARK

A PAIR of larks built their nest and hatched out their young in a field of growing corn. One evening, when the young were nearly ready to fly, the farmer who owned the field came into it with his son.

" This corn," said he, " is ready to cut. Let

us ask our friends to come here early to-morrow and help us."

The young larks heard what he said, and, as soon as their mother came back with food, they screamed all together :

" The man said that he was coming with his friends early to-morrow to reap the corn. If we do not go, we shall all be cut into pieces."

" There is no hurry," said the lark. " If he counts on the help of others, there will be no reaping to-morrow ; so let us have a good meal and go to sleep."

The lark was right. No one came next morning. In the evening the farmer again appeared with his son.

" This corn must be cut," he said. " Go and beg all our relatives to be here without fail to-morrow morning, for it is clear we cannot count on our friends."

The young larks heard this, and were very excited and frightened.

" He is coming to-morrow with all his relatives," they screamed, as soon as they saw their mother.

" Is that all ? " said she. " If he is still counting on the help of others, there is nothing to be frightened about. Let us have a good meal and go to sleep."

Next morning no one came, and in the evening the farmer again appeared with his son, and said :

" This corn must not remain uncut one day longer. As we cannot count on others to help us, we must do the work as best we can ourselves, with the family and our own labourers."

When the mother lark heard that, she said :

" If they are going to do the work themselves, then it is time to go."

That same evening they went ; nothing was left behind but an empty nest ; and next day the corn was cut.

37. THE CROW'S MISTAKE

A CROW saw an eagle swoop down upon a flock of sheep, pick up a lamb with his claws, and carry it off with ease.

" Why should I not do the same ? " said the crow ; " it seems quite simple."

Rising into the air, he also swooped down upon the flock, just like the eagle. He then drove his claws into the woolly back of a fine fat lamb, and tried to rise into the air. He flapped his wings, and flapped again ; it was of no use—he could not rise an inch. The lamb seemed hardly to know he was on its back.

At last the crow saw that he had made a mistake. He gave up trying to fly away with the lamb, only to find that he could not fly away at all, for his claws were fast caught in the thick wool of the lamb's back.

There he remained till the shepherd saw him and pulled him off. He was put in a cage to amuse the shepherd's children.

" What kind of a bird is he ? " asked one of the children.

" He thought himself an eagle," answered the shepherd ; " he has now found out that he is only a crow."

38. THE MONKEY AND THE DOLPHIN

A SHIP sailing to Piræus, the port of Athens, was caught in a storm and sent to the bottom. The sailors were left struggling in the waves, and with them a pet monkey they had on board.

Some dolphins, who were swimming by, came to the rescue of the sailors, and carried them to Piræus. One of them saw the monkey and, taking him for a man, let him climb on his back. As the dolphin swam towards Piræus, he asked the monkey whether he was an Athenian.

" Certainly I am," replied the monkey, and, flattered at being taken for a man, he added, " I belong to one of the noblest families in the town."

" I suppose," said the dolphin, " you know Piræus very well."

" Of course I do," said the monkey ; " he is one of my best friends."

The dolphin laughed at the mistake, and looking up saw, for the first time, that he was carrying a monkey. Annoyed at the creature's conceit, he dived, leaving the other to get ashore as best he could.

39. THE ASS IN THE LION'S SKIN

An ass, having heard a lion roar, felt sure that he could roar just as well. He put on a lion's skin and walked about making the most furious braying. Everybody, on seeing and hearing him, fled for their lives. The ass was much pleased with himself, and very much amused.

He met his master coming round a corner, and roared louder than ever. His master was turning to run when he noticed something about the roaring that he seemed to have heard before. He took a second look at the ass, and noticed one of his ears sticking up out of an opening in the lion's skin.

That was enough. A few seconds later the lion's skin was off the ass's back, and a shower of blows was falling on it ; he paid dearly for pretending to be something he was not.

40. KILLING THE GOOSE WITH THE GOLDEN EGGS

A certain man was lucky enough to have a goose that laid a golden egg every day. He had only

" I cannot wait."

to go to its nest, and there was the egg, all shining gold, and solid gold right through.

The man turned the golden eggs into money ; he was rich, but he wished to get richer, and all at once.

"I cannot wait till that old bird has laid as many eggs as I need. I shall have to wait for weeks. I want them now, at once."

The man killed the goose, and cut her open, expecting to find in her a number of golden eggs. He found none.

41. THE BEAR GIVES A LESSON

Two hunters learned that a big bear had been seen in the woods. They wanted some money, so they went to a dealer in furs and offered him the skin, telling him that it was one of the finest skins ever seen.

"But you have not got the skin," said the dealer.

"It is as good as in our hands," answered the hunters; "in two days it will be in your hands."

"When it is in my hands I will pay you, not sooner," said the dealer.

The hunters had to be content with that. Off they went. After going many miles into the woods, they came suddenly upon the bear, an enormous beast and very savage. It gave a growl and rushed at them.

One dropped his gun and scrambled up a tree; he did not stop till he was near the top, where he felt sure that the bear could not follow because of its weight.

The bear came up to him.

The other threw himself flat on the ground, made his body stiff, and held his breath. He had read somewhere that bears do not touch a dead body.

The bear came up to him and smelt him, turned him over with its snout, and, thinking him dead, went off, after stopping to glance up the tree at the other man, who nearly fell down with fright.

When the bear had quite gone, the man in the

tree slid down and went to his friend, half expecting to find him really dead.

" The bear has gone," he said ; " you have had a lucky escape. The bear's jaws came so close to you, I wondered what he whispered in your ear."

" I will tell you," said the other. " He whispered that it is very foolish to sell a bear's skin before you have killed your bear."

42. THE OAK AND THE REED

ONE day the oak said to the reed : " I feel sorry for you ; it is a pity you are so weak ; you seem unable to bear even the weight of the tiny wren, and the lightest puff of air makes you bend. Look at me. A tempest hurts me no more than a breeze. If you were closer to me, instead of living in the mud and water, I would gladly protect you with my strength."

" Your pity," said the reed, " is needless. The tempest has no terror for me ; when it comes I bend, but I do not break. You cannot bend, but you may break."

Hardly had it spoken when a tempest arose. The oak held good ; the reed bent. The tempest doubled its fury. Still the reed bent, but the oak was torn up by the roots.

43. PRIDE GOES BEFORE A FALL

" Out of my way, wretched insect." Thus spoke the lion, in his pride, to the gnat, who at once declared war.

" Do you think," cried he, " that your title of king makes me frightened ? An ox is stronger than you, yet I can do what I like with him."

Buzzing with anger, the gnat rose in the air, shot down on to the lion, and stung him—now in the back, now on his muzzle, now right inside his nostrils, and now in his ear.

The lion roared, he bit the air, he struck out with his paws, he lashed his tail, rolled on the ground, and tore at his own flesh. It was all of no use; he never even saw his foe. He ended by sinking to the ground, worn out by rage.

The gnat flew off, singing a song of victory. So blinded by pride was he that he did not see a spider's web stretched across his path. Into it he flew ; and thus, within a few moments, the conqueror of the King of Beasts became the victim of the humble spider.

44. THE MISERY OF MIDAS

Long ago there lived a great Greek king called Midas. He had the good fortune to be of service to the god Bacchus, who was so pleased that he granted Midas any wish that he liked. Now Midas loved, above all, riches. Without stopping to think, he said :

" Grant me that anything I touch may be turned into gold."

" I grant it," said Bacchus.

Midas lost no time in touching things. He began with a stone ; it became a lump of gold in his hand. He was delighted. He plucked an apple ; and at once in his hand lay a golden apple. He touched all the things he could see. Every touch made shining gold. He laughed with joy. He was so delighted that he gave a feast.

There never was such a feast ! Hundreds of guests were invited. The king appeared in a dress of shining gold ; and when he reached the head of the table, he passed his hand over his carved oak chair, and it became a golden throne. The guests shouted with wonder and delight.

Then Midas raised to his lips a glass of sparkling wine. The glass became gold in his hand; but that was not all. The moment it touched his lips and mouth the sparkling wine also became gold.

The king dropped the cup. He was filled with fear and horror. Did that mean that all his food and drink were to become gold ? For a while he stood trembling among his silent, staring guests.

Then in haste he touched a piece of bread ; it also turned to gold. All the food he touched turned to gold, even the water he put to his lips.

The feast did not take place. The guests went without being told to go ; and as they went they snatched what food they could. Some were sorry for the king ; others said it was his own fault ; others thought it funny, and laughed.

Midas himself stood thinking. He saw that there was only one thing to do. He prayed to Bacchus to take back the wish. Bacchus agreed to do so, but he had made up his mind to give the king a lesson ; so he told him he could be free from his wish, but only if he went up along a certain river and bathed in the spring where it began.

Midas went. It was a dreadful journey, for the road was rough and the king was hungry and thirsty. The sight of the water close beside him made him thirstier still.

At last, with sore feet and tired legs, he got to the spring. He bathed in the cool, clear water, and a few seconds later he was pouring it down his throat. He liked it better than all the gold in the world.

From that day, Midas hated gold and riches. He lived very simply, and found himself all the happier and healthier.

45. THE MILLER GOES TO MARKET

AN old miller and his son, a boy of twelve, were driving their donkey to market in order to sell it. On the way, they met some girls.

" Just look there ! " cried one of the girls, pointing to the miller and his son. " Did you ever see such foolish people ? They go tramping along on a hot day like this when they might be riding on their donkey."

" You're right," said another ; " the biggest donkey of the three is not the one with long ears."

On hearing that, the old miller put his boy on the donkey, and walked along beside him.

They passed an inn. Some old men were seated on the bench outside in the sun ; they were arguing.

" There," said one of them, " now look at that : the boy rides, the poor old father has to walk. It just proves what I was saying. There is no respect for old age in these days. I call it wicked."

" So it is," said the others.

The miller overheard their talk ; he made his son walk, and got up himself.

A few minutes later they met a number of women and children coming from market.

" Why, you lazy old man," shouted several voices at once, " how can you have the heart to

ride like a bishop while your poor little boy tries
to keep up with you on foot ? "

The miller told the boy to get up behind him.
On went the ass with its two riders.

After a while they met a man who stopped and
eyed them sternly.

" May I ask if that donkey is your own ? "
said he.

" Yes," answered the miller.

" Indeed ? " said the man. " Well, allow me
to remark that I should not have thought so
from the way you treat it. If you make it carry
you two another mile, its back will break. However, it is no business of mine whether you break
its back or not. I bid you good-day."

With another stern look, he passed on.

The miller, afraid that he might already have
injured the donkey, tied its legs together and
fastened them to a pole. Then he and the boy,
each with one end of the pole on his shoulder,
carried the beast between them.

Everybody they met laughed at them. When
they were crossing a bridge the donkey, hating to
be tied up, managed to kick itself free, but in
falling off the pole it fell into the river and was
drowned.

46. BELLING THE CAT

A CERTAIN cat named Rodilard killed so many
rats that those left hardly dared to leave their
holes. But to stay in their holes was to starve.
What was to be done ? The rats met to talk
over this question one evening, when Rodilard
was out enjoying himself.

An old rat opened the discussion.

" Our subject, my friends, is Rodilard."

" Down with Rodilard ! " cried the other rats.
" Death to Rodilard ! "

Old Rat. Oh yes ! You shout " Death to
Rodilard ! " but you know well enough that
Rodilard will not die. He always has been ; he
always will be.

Other Rats. It is true. He always has been ;
he always will be.

Old Rat. Then what is to be done ?

Other Rats. Nothing can be done.

Old Rat. I say that something can be done.
I know a way of saving us from Rodilard. [*Loud
applause, after which the old Rat continued.*]
See this bell ? Well it must be tied to the neck
of Rodilard. Why ? Because it will ring every
time he moves ; we shall know when he is
coming, and when he comes we shall not be
there ! "

Other Rats. Splendid ! We shall not be there !
Ha, ha ! We shall not be there ! "

Old Rat. Now, my friends, we have to find
some one to tie the bell to the neck of Rodilard.
That can, of course, be done when he is asleep.

Other Rats. Yes, we have only to find some
one . . . yes, to find some one . . . yes, some
one . . . some one . . . yes.

Old Rat. Now, which of you will tie this bell
to the neck of Rodilard ?

Other Rats [*each to the others*]. Yes, which of you . . . of you . . . which . . . ?

Old Rat. Once more I ask, which of you will bell that cat ?

" Yes, which ? " asked a soft, purring voice at the open window. There stood Rodilard, a hungry glare in his green eyes. The old rat dropped the bell and sprang, head first, into his hole. The others followed, but not before Rodilard, with a fierce spring, had caught two— one with each paw.

47. THE SAUSAGE

A WOODMAN was about to cut down an old oak when out of it jumped a wood-goddess. She begged him to spare the tree ; it was her home. He consented, and as a reward the goddess promised to grant three wishes to him and his wife.

That evening the pair sat long by the fire, thinking what was to be the first wish.

" The first thing to wish for," said the wife, " is riches."

" No," said the man ; " what is the use of riches, if you die ? The first thing to wish for is long life."

" Yes ; but that can be the second wish. Let us make sure of the riches. What is the use of long life without riches ? "

They went on arguing and arguing. The woodman, who was feeling tired and hungry, said at last :

" I wish I had a good, large pork sausage to eat."

The words were hardly out of his mouth when a good, large pork sausage, beautifully cooked, lay on the table in front of him.

" Oh, you foolish man ! " cried the wife. " You and your wretched sausage ! I wish it were stuck to your nose."

Next moment the sausage *was* stuck to his nose. However much he pulled and tugged, it remained stuck. Nor could he cut it off without cutting his nose.

" I'm not going to spend the rest of my life with a sausage hanging from my nose," said he angrily ; and then he shouted : " I wish this sausage gone."

It went.

That was the last of the three wishes.

48. CHANTICLEER AND THE FOX

CHANTICLEER, the barn-cock, was crowing merrily in the yard, while his hens were having a dust-bath. He was standing by a cabbage patch. Seeing a butterfly on one of the cabbages, he turned to catch it, when he saw something else that made him stretch up his neck and utter a startled " Kok! Kok! Kok!"

What he saw was a fox, lying flat and looking at him with his yellow eyes. Chanticleer would have flown away at once, but the fox said :

" My good sir, why go ? Why be afraid ? I am your friend. I have come here just to listen to your merry song, for you have a voice as fine as any angel's voice in heaven. Let me tell you I knew both your father and your mother."

" Did you really ? " said Chanticleer.

" Yes ; they have both been into my house, and were very welcome. Never did I hear any one sing as your father did in the morning. I noticed how he had to close his eyes tight, so loud he sang, while at the same time he rose upon his toes and stretched his neck up high. So sang your father. Let me see if, in very truth, you are his son."

Then Chanticleer stood upon his toes, stretched his neck up high, and began to crow with his eyes tight shut. At once the fox started up, caught him by the throat, and carried him on his back toward the wood.

When the hens saw their Chanticleer being carried away, they filled the yard with cackling. Out came their mistress and her daughters. They cried out upon the fox, and after him they ran, and with them Coll, their dog. After them ran the neighbours, and their dogs, with shouting and barking; then cow, and calf, and hogs; then ducks, and geese, and swarms of bees.

They all went after the fox, and with such a storm of noise it seemed as if the sky would crack and fall.

Chanticleer, lying upon the fox's back, said:

"Sir, allow me to say that if I were you, I should turn upon this stupid, noisy crowd and cry, 'Be off, you foolish rogues! This fowl is mine; I mean to eat him; I will eat him, in spite of you.'"

The fox answered: "Right, I will do it." And as he opened his jaws to speak those words, the cock broke away and flew into a tree.

"Alas!" said the fox. "Listen, dear Chanticleer, I know I did wrong to snatch you from that yard, but, sir, I really meant no harm; it was all my fun. Come down, and I will explain more fully."

"Not I," replied Chanticleer. "May I be burnt alive if you deceive me more than once. Once bitten, twice shy."

49. THE COLT'S LESSON

A HORSE and a colt lived in a meadow in which there was everything a horse could want—good grass, fresh water, shade and shelter.

The colt stuffed himself with food every day,

took very little exercise, and rested without being tired. He grew fat ; he felt ill, and he was bored.

Finally he went to his father, the horse, and said :

"The grass of this meadow upsets me, the clover is tasteless, the water undrinkable, and the air stifling. In short, I shall die unless we leave this frightful place."

"Very well," said the horse, "where shall we go ?"

"Oh, anywhere."

"All right. Let us go just straight ahead."

They went straight ahead. They came to the slope of a mountain, and up it they went. Evening came, and there was nothing to eat but a little coarse, dry grass, and little to drink.

Next day they went down the mountain slope. There was still less to eat and drink. The colt was so hungry and thirsty that he could scarcely drag one foot after another.

At the foot of the mountain they entered a wild, rocky valley. The colt was glad to eat the leaves of a few small bushes, and to drink water muddied by mountain sheep.

Another evening came. The horse took a sudden turn to the left. They walked, and then slept a little, then walked on again in the moonlight. While it was still dark they found themselves on the edge of what looked like a meadow.

There was good grass round their feet, and near by a pool of water.

"What lovely grass!" said the colt. "What clover! What water! Never have I drunk such perfect water; and the air here makes one want to gallop and jump and neigh with joy. This is the place for us. Let us stay here always."

"Certainly," said the horse.

Day began to break; the sun rose and chased away the darkness and the mist from the meadow.

The colt looked round, and was astonished to find himself in the very same meadow he had left two days before.

The horse had made the round on purpose, to show the colt that the fault was not in the meadow but in the colt himself.

50. THE SELFISH FRIEND

Two friends were walking along a road in the moonlight. One of them saw lying on the ground a purse full of money. He picked it up and put it into his pocket. The other said:

"Well, that is a piece of good luck for us."

"For *us*, no!" said the first. "For *me*, yes!"

The other said no more. They walked on. As they were passing through a wood they were attacked by thieves. The friend with the purse stood trembling with fear, unable to move. He cried :

"We are lost ! "

"Not *we*," said the other. "But *you*, yes ! " Being quick of foot, he escaped.

The thieves got the purse.

51. THE CORRIDOR OF TEMPTATION

A KING wanted a new treasurer, some one to look after his treasures and all his money matters. The last treasurer had been put in prison because he had been dishonest ; he had taken for himself large sums of money.

"How am I to make sure of getting some one really honest ? " asked the king of his prime minister.

"I think I can find a way," said the prime minister.

"Very good," said the king, " I leave it to you."

On the day fixed all the persons who offered themselves for the post of treasurer came to the palace. They were all put together in one room. Each one left the room by himself, and passed through a long passage or corridor, which led into a hall. When all had arrived in the hall, they were made to stand in a line facing the king.

The prime minister then said a few words to them, and told them that the king would choose as treasurer that one who danced the best.

"Danced the best!" cried the king. "What on earth for? What has dancing to do with looking after my treasures?"

"I will show you," answered the prime minister, "that it has a great deal to do with your treasures." Then he turned to the would-be treasurers and said: "Now, my friends, I must ask you all to be good enough to begin."

They danced. All of them, except one, danced very badly; they seemed as if they were carrying some great weight which prevented them from lifting their feet. They soon became tired—excepting one. He went on dancing, flinging his legs about, waving his arms, leaping into the air, and ending on his knees before the king.

"This is an honest man," said the prime minister; "and now I will show you why I think so."

He made a sign to the attendants. They went up to the dancers and slit open their clothes with scissors. Out from each of them poured a shower of gold coins that rolled all over the floor.

"Each one of these gentlemen passed down that long corridor before entering this hall," continued the prime minister; "each of them was alone in the corridor. In it was a chest full of gold addressed to the king's treasury. By my orders it was left shut, but unlocked. As you see, each helped himself to so much gold that he could hardly lift his feet. Only one passed through the corridor without being tempted. Are you ready to take him on trial as your treasurer ? "

" I am ready to give him a trial," said the king. " But what about these rascals ? "

" Let them go," answered the prime minister ; " they have been punished enough."

52. THE WOLF WHO WAS AT OXFORD

ONE day the wolf and the fox were out together looking for something to eat. In a field they saw a mare grazing. With her was a beautiful little colt.

" What a good meal that colt would make," said the fox.

" You are right," said the wolf. " What is more, that colt shall make our meal, or my name is not wolf. Go and say to the mare from me that I, the wolf, wish to buy the colt."

The fox did as he was told.

The mare had been watching the pair out of the corner of her eye ; she knew all about them. She answered that she would be happy to sell her colt.

" At what price ? " asked the fox.

" You will find the price marked on the sole of one of my hind feet."

The fox took one glance at the mare's hind feet and replied :

" I am sorry to say that I do not know how to read. I am only the messenger of the wolf. He is a great scholar. I will tell him what you say."

" Right," said the mare. " Let him come and read for himself, if he can."

When the wolf heard the reply, he said :

" Can I read, did she ask ? Of course I can read. Was I not at Oxford ? Did I not learn to read English there, and Latin and Greek, and Hebrew and other languages, ancient and modern ? Can I read, did she say ? She is going to see if I can read. Just you wait."

" Certainly," said the fox, settling himself down with an evil grin to see what was going to happen.

The wolf went up to the mare, and asked to see the sole marked with the price. The mare raised one of her hind feet and, at the same time, gave the wolf a kick that broke most of his teeth and sent him off howling.

53. THE WOLF HAS A LESSON IN FISHING

THE wolf was out hunting. It was winter, the ground was frozen, the ponds and streams were covered with ice. The wolf ran along, hoping to find something to eat, for he was starving.

On entering a field near a farmhouse he met Renard the fox, whom he hated. Renard knew how the wolf felt, so he took good care to keep a few yards between them. They both pretended to be very much pleased to see each other.

" All the good wishes of the season to you, dear friend," said the fox.

" The same to you," said the wolf, " and I hope you may never feel as hungry as I do now ; I could eat anything—even a fox," he added to himself, moving a few steps nearer to Renard.

The fox moved a few steps back, and as he did so there came into his mind a way of playing a trick on the wolf. He said :

" Do you like fish ? There are plenty in that pond over there."

" Yes, I know that there are fish in that pond," answered the wolf, " but how can one catch them ? "

" It is simple enough," answered the fox. " Come along and I will show you."

They ran to the pond, the fox being careful to keep his distance from the wolf. They found the pond frozen over.

" How on earth can I catch fish with that ice on the water ? " growled the wolf. " Are you trying to make fun of me ? "

" I would not dare to make fun of you," said the

fox. " Listen, and I will tell you what to do.
Look at this little hole in the ice. It is just big
enough for you to slip your tail through ; my
tail is too bushy."

" Why should I slip my tail through ? "

" Because," said the fox, " fish are very
curious ; they will want to know what your tail
means, and whether it is good to eat ; they will
nibble at it, and their mouths will get caught in
the hairs. Then you will only have to pull them
out."

" I see," said the wolf. " And what do you
expect to get out of this, Renard ? "

" I shall get out of it only what you care to
give me."

" Well, that is true enough," said the wolf.
Then he set about pushing his tail through the
hole, while the fox stood by watching him with
a grin, for he knew what was going to happen.

After the wolf had been sitting on the ice, with
his tail in the water, for about a minute, he
grew tired and said :

" I do not think much of your way of fishing ;
not a fish has nibbled."

" You must be patient," said the fox. " I
have seen fishermen sit for hours waiting ; you
have only waited for one minute."

The wolf went on sitting, while the fox talked
of this and that to make the time seem shorter.

" Still not a nibble," said the wolf at last.

"Let me have a look," said the fox. He went up to the hole and saw, as he expected, that the water in it had frozen hard round the tail. Then he gave the wolf a sudden bite in the back.

The wolf uttered a howl of rage, and tried to turn and spring upon the fox. But he found himself tied by the tail to the ice.

The fox enjoyed himself. First he sat down and told the wolf all that he thought about him; then he kept making rushes at him from behind and snapping.

The wolf howled with fury. He made such a noise that the farmer heard him and looked out to find what was the matter. Seeing the wolf, he snatched up his gun and ran toward the pond.

The fox made off. The wolf struggled hard to free his tail. While he was doing so, a charge of shot struck him and made him leap free into the air. He left most of the skin and hair of his tail behind in the ice, and went off snarling with rage and pain.

54. THE LION, THE WOLF, AND THE FOX

THE lion, the wolf, and the fox went out hunting together. The fox and the wolf ran forward scouting, while the lion followed at a slower pace. They came upon a bull, a cow, and a little calf.

The lion killed the bull, the wolf the cow, while the fox made short work of the little calf.

"Now," said the lion, "we must divide the prey. Perhaps the wolf will tell us what he thinks is a fair division."

"Certainly," said the wolf. "Nothing simpler. You, of course, must have the bull ; the cow is for me ; and, as for Renard, the calf will do well enough for him. That is the best division one could have."

"Is it ?" said the lion, and he gave the wolf a blow that nearly broke his jaw and made him howl with pain.

The lion then turned to the fox, and said he would be pleased, very pleased to have Renard's ideas on the question of the division of the prey.

"I propose," said the fox, with a pleasant smile, "that Your Majesty should have the bull ; that her Gracious Majesty, the lioness, should have the cow, and that the calf should go to our handsome and charming prince, the lion cub."

"That is a fine division," said the lion. "What made you judge so wisely, Renard ?"

"The wolf's jaw, Your Majesty."

55. TOO CLEVER BY HALF

A FOX and a cat were talking of the ways they had of escaping from their enemies.

" I have dozens of ways," said the fox ; " when one fails, I try another."

" Yes, you think yourself very clever," said the cat. " I have only one way, but it is better than all yours put together."

" Well, we shall soon see about that," replied the fox, " for here comes a pack of dogs."

The cat sprang up into the tree and stayed there, hidden among the leaves. The fox went off at a run, with the dogs upon his scent. Before the end of the day he had tried every trick he could think of. In the end he was run down and killed. He died at the foot of the tree, where the cat still crouched, hidden and safe.

56. THE TORTOISE TRAVELS

A TORTOISE wished to travel. She spoke of the matter to two ducks, and they agreed to carry her over the world.

" How are you going to carry me ? " asked the tortoise.

" It is quite simple," answered one of the ducks. " Here is a stick. You get hold of the middle of it with your jaws, we get hold of each end, and then off we go."

No sooner said than done. The two ducks flew through the air with the tortoise hanging by its teeth from the stick. They were a strange sight. The people down below gazed up, astonished, and cried :

"Look up there! It must be the queen of tortoises travelling through the sky."

They laughed and cheered. The tortoise, who did not think there was anything to laugh at, opened her jaws and cried out :

"I am just as good as a queen . . ."

She said so much, and no more.

I wonder why.

57. THE HORSE-CLOTH

A RICH merchant had a son whom he wished to see married to the daughter of a knight. The knight was not very eager to allow the marriage ; he consented to it at last, but only if the merchant gave the whole of his fortune to his son on the day of the marriage. The merchant agreed.

For some years after the marriage the old merchant lived in his son's house. He had not a penny beyond what his son gave him, but he was happy with little. He found his joy in watching his grandchildren grow up and in playing with them. The children were very fond of him.

But as time passed, the son's wife came more and more to dislike the old man ; she wanted him driven out of the house, and would have been glad to see him go with nothing but the clothes he wore. She kept on asking her husband to do what she asked, till at last he gave in, and he told his father he must go.

The old merchant, of course, did not want to go. He said :

" Cannot I live somewhere in the garden or courtyard ? A shed to sleep in, and a little food every day—that is all I need."

His son answered :

" You know quite well that it is not I who want you to go, but go you must—right away from this house."

" Very well," said the old man, " but give me a cloak to keep me warm."

" I have no cloak to give you."

" May I not have a horse-cloth ? "

The young man began to feel ashamed. He told his son, a boy of about ten, to fetch a horse-cloth for his grandfather from the stable.

The boy said nothing ; he went to the stable and brought back the horse-cloth, after cutting it into halves.

" Why," asked his grandfather, " have you done that ? Your father gave me the whole cloth ; you give me half ! You are worse than he."

" Give your grandfather the whole cloth," said the father sternly.

" I will not," said the boy.

" Why not ? " asked the father.

" Because," answered the boy, " I am keeping

one half for you. When you are old, I will treat you just as you have treated your own father."

The old merchant lived on in peace in the house, thanks to the courage and ready wit of his grandson.

58. THE TWO FRIENDS

Two dogs sat talking in the sun outside the kitchen door. They talked and they talked, now of one thing, now of another. Among the things they talked of was friendship.

" How fine it is," said one of them, " to live with a trusted friend, to help him in trouble, to make him happy, to fight for him. That is what I feel about our friendship."

" I feel the same, dear friend," said the other. " That is why it is so foolish of us to fight each other, as we sometimes do. Why fight ? How silly ! There is plenty of room and food for both of us. Let us show that dogs can be even better friends than men."

" Right," cried the first. " Come, give me your paw, and let us swear everlasting friendship."

They grasped each other's paws, they licked each other's faces, they wept for joy—when out of the kitchen window a bone came flying.

No sooner did the bone reach the ground than both dogs were upon it ; they bit and growled, they screamed and rolled and pushed. In the end they were separated by the cook with a bucketful of cold water.

THE END

QUESTIONS

THE following questions can be used either for class or individual work. Most of the fables can be, and have been, acted in the classroom.

1. If you had been the thin cat, would you have gone again to the palace ? What would you have done to escape another blow ?

2. Tell how the hare made the lion kill himself.

3. Put in your own words the two lines made by the deer.
   Who was the friend in need in this fable ?

4. What was the first thing the bear did to keep the fly off the man's face ? Why did it fail ? What was the second ? Why did that fail ? What was the third ? Why did the man forgive the bear for hurting him ?

5. The monkey " kept his head." What does that mean ?

6. What was the real reason that made the potter ride against the enemy ? Why did the enemy run ? Why did not the potter go prancing along the road on a horse ? Why do we call him lucky ?

7. If the jackal was small and weak, in what way was he better than the alligator ?

8. Read again from " They went on and met a jackal " to the end. How did the jackal get the tiger back into the cage ?

9. What were the four useful things the partridge told the man ? Why did it tell him the fourth ? When did the man *not* stop to think ?

10. Who built the hut in the wood ? Why ? " The neighbour guessed easily what the merchant meant." What did he mean ?

11. Why was the gardener foolish ?
  " A little knowledge is a dangerous thing." Give an example of this from the story.

12. How did the crane get the fish to leave their pool ? Why did he not eat the crab ?

13. If the rabbit and weasel had come to you to judge their dispute, to whom would you have given the hole ? Why ?

14. Why was the rat wiser than the rabbit and the weasel of fable 13 ? Why was the rat wise not to trust the cat ?

15. Tell the story of the three rogues.

16. Why had the judge many enemies ? What did they say about him the first time ? What did they say then ? Finish the story.

17. Which, do you think, gave the right answer about the feasts ? Why do you think that ?

18. Which, do you think, was the stupid one ? Why ?

19. Why did the heron end by eating a slug ?

20. Make up a story in which one child gets some sweets from another by flattery. Did the barn-cock really see a dog coming ? Why did he say he did ?

21. Why did the fox serve the soup on a flat dish ? Why did the storks serve the chicken in a narrow-necked pot ?

22. Why did the hare start so late ?

23. Read again what the milkmaid said ; and then say all that she hoped to do with the money.

24. What did the wolf like even better than plenty of food ?

25. Why did the god punish the second woodsman ?

26. What was there good in the ant, and what was there

bad ? What good thing had the grasshopper
done ? Which do you like the better ?

27. Why did the wolf try to find an excuse for killing
the lamb ?

28. What was bad in the behaviour of both the wolf and
the stork ?

29. Read again the fourth paragraph. Why was the
lion amused ? Why was he amused still more ?
What happened afterwards ?

30. Why would not the fox help the goat out ? Why
did the fox not want to be found by the villagers ?

31. What would you have done if you had been the god ?

32. Why did no footprints point outward ?

33. When you say " Sour grapes " to some one, what do
you mean ?

34. What fault did the frog have ?

35. Read again the two paragraphs beginning with
" *When the next spring came* " and " *While he sat*,"
and then say why the eggs were put in Jupiter's
lap, and what happened.

36. Read the last two paragraphs again. Say in what
way the lark was wise.

37. What was the crow's mistake ?

38. What mistake did the monkey make about Piræus ?
What did the dolphin learn from the mistake ?
What did he do ?

39. In what way was the ass like the monkey in fable
38 ? In what way did each pay for his folly ?

40. Tell the story.

41. In what way were the two hunters like the milkmaid in fable 23 ?

42. How was it the reed was still standing after the
storm, while the oak was torn up by the roots ?

43. Tell how both the lion and the gnat fell because of
pride. What goes before a fall ?

44. How did Midas come to hate gold ?

45. Finish " In trying to please every one the miller pleaded . . ."
46. Finish " It is easier to talk than to . . ."
47. Tell the story.
48. When the fox said that Chanticleer's parents had been into his house, and were very welcome, what did he really mean ? Why did he say that Chanticleer's father used to shut his eyes when he sang ? Why did Chanticleer sing, and why did the fox let him go ?
49. What was the fault in the colt ?
50. Tell the story.
51. Why did the prime minister put the chest of gold in the corridor ? Why did he make the would-be treasurers dance ?
52. What fault had the wolf ? What do you think of the fox's behaviour ?
53. What was the trick that the fox played on the wolf ? What excuse had he for playing this trick ?
54. Which division do you think the better—that of the fox or the wolf ? Why do you think that ?
55. Imagine a story where the cat's one way of escape would not be better than the fox's many ways.
56. What fault had the tortoise ?
57. Why did the old merchant live on in the house ?
58. What ought the dogs to have done ?

PRINTED IN GREAT BRITAIN AT
THE PRESS OF THE PUBLISHERS

STORY BOOKS IN THE JUNIOR
"Teaching of English"
SERIES

No. 73. THE WATER BABIES.

by CHARLES KINGSLEY.

The Editor has succeeded in skilfully detaching the story of Tom and Ellie from the mass of matter which makes Kingsley's tale in its complete form somewhat wearisome to younger children.

The book concludes with a set of Questions designed to draw out all the human and literary qualities of the story.

No. 126. HEIDI.

by JOHANNA SPYRI.

translated by LOUISE BROOKS.

This story of a little Swiss girl and her relations with the world of Nature and of Man makes the best possible reading for Junior Girls.

The Louise Brooks translation has been slightly but very carefully modified for English readers. Teachers who do not know this book are strongly recommended to use it for home or holiday reading, or for silent reading in class.

No. 74. THE FLYING TRUNK and Other Stories.

by HANS ANDERSEN.

The selected stories are : The Flying Trunk ; The Emperor's New Clothes ; The Storks ; The Darning Needle ; The Swineherd ; The Little Match Girl ; The Garden of Paradise ; Ole Luk-Oie ; Little Ida's Flowers ; Little Thumb ; and Five Out of One Shell.

The stories are followed by a section entitled " On Thinking it Over," containing questions and suggestions for further study.

No. 138. THE QUEEN BEE and Other Nature Tales.

by CARL EWALD.

These beautiful Nature Tales, by the Danish author who has " succeeded " Hans Andersen, are translated into English by Professor G. C. Moore Smith. They are very fully and beautifully illustrated.

No. 70. THE FAIRY BOOK. Part I.

by MRS. CRAIK.

This volume, which is printed in large, clear type, contains the following stories : The Sleeping Beauty ; Hop-o'-my-Thumb ; Cinderella ; John Dietrich ; Beauty and the Beast ; Little One Eye ; Jack the Giant Killer ; Tom Thumb ; and Rumpelstilzchen.

At the end of the book is a set of Questions designed to recall the most interesting points in each story.

No. 113. THE FAIRY BOOK. Part II.

by MRS. CRAIK.

This volume contains the stories of : Fortunatus ; The Bremen Town Musicians ; Riquet with the Tuft ; House Island ; Snow-white and Rose-red ; Jack and the Bean-Stalk ; Graciosa and Percinet ; The Iron Stove ; and The Woodcutter's Daughter.

Mrs. Craik's retelling of these old stories is excellently done, none of the imaginative qualities being obscured.